PROTECTING
HIS WITNESS

KATIE REUS

*****

Katie Reus

Praise for the novels of Katie Reus

Alpha Instinct is a wild, hot ride for readers. The story grabs you and doesn't let go. —*New York Times* bestselling author, Cynthia Eden

"Sinful, Sexy, Suspense... Katie Reus pulls you in and never lets go." —*New York Times* bestselling author, Laura Wright

"His Secret Past was an action packed page turner." —Night Owl Reviews

*"...*No One to Trust was a fast-paced, steamy romantic suspense with quite a bit of emotional depth. I would recommend it to any fan of the genre." —RR&H Novel Thoughts & Book Talk

"I couldn't put this book down. This was the whole package for me and I can't wait to read more of this author's books. This is definitely a book I will read again!" —Secrets of a Book Lover

"Explosive danger and enough sexual tension to set the pages on fire . . . fabulous!" —*New York Times* bestselling author, Alexandra Ivy

"Sexy alphas, kick-ass heroines, and twisted villains will keep you turning the pages . . . a winner." — Caridad Piñeiro, *New York Times* bestselling author

"Nonstop action, a solid plot, good pacing and riveting suspense..." —*RT Book Reviews (4.5 Stars)*

Seven years ago she broke his heart...

Leaving Vincent was the hardest thing Jordan Alvarado ever had to do, but she had no choice. She never expected to come back, or for the smoldering attraction between them to ignite into a bonfire. But deep down, she knows he'll never be able to understand or forgive what she did, and that being with him will only lead to heartbreak.

He's not letting her go again...

Former SEAL Vincent Hansen never got over Jordan and the way she up and left him without a trace. When she reappears and explains what happened, he's even more furious. He doesn't know what he wants from her, but when she's targeted in a series of potentially deadly attacks, he realizes he's never stopped loving her. Now he'll do whatever it takes to keep her safe and convince her that she was always meant to be his.

Dedication

For my husband, who puts up with my crazy hours and
is the best support system anyone could ask for.
Thank you.

Prologue

Jordan Alvarado shut the door to her Jeep and tossed her backpack into the backseat as she settled against the driver's seat. She'd just picked up her weekly paycheck at the off campus bookstore where she worked and had the next couple days off. She still couldn't believe she was finally done with college. Well, for now. After four years at UC San Diego she was done with all her classes and would be graduating next weekend—summa cum laude, thank you very much—with a degree in early education. She planned to go back for her Master's but for now, she just wanted to celebrate that she had her degree and could finally start a job in a field she loved.

She couldn't wait to celebrate with her boyfriend, Vincent.

Boyfriend.

That still felt too surreal and didn't seem quite an accurate word for the man who had stolen her heart.

Completely by accident too. For almost four years of college she'd had pretty much no interest in dating. She'd been attracted to some of her classmates, sure, but her class load and the fact that she was on multiple scholarships left little time for dating. Keeping her grades up had been necessary. She had a lot of friends and preferred to hang out with her girlfriends anyway.

Speaking of…her phone buzzed, alerting her to a text message as she started her engine. She smiled when she saw Vincent's name on the screen.

Vincent: Hey babe, where r u?

Jordan: Leaving work, u at my place yet?

Vincent: No, having drinks w/ an old navy friend, might be out late. Unless u want me to head over now?

Jordan: No, have fun. Let yourself in if I'm asleep.

Vincent: U can join us. I want to show u off.

Laughing to herself, she shook her head. He was such a caveman sometimes. Normally she'd love to meet up with him, but she was beyond exhausted.

Jordan: Tired from work, but next time for sure.

Vincent: Ok, love u.

Jordan: Love u too.

Vincent: Miss u.

She smiled at the last text. *Jordan: Always. Now go enjoy your friend!*

She and Vincent had been so consumed with each other the past few months that she wanted him to spend time with his friends, especially since he'd be leaving California soon.

That thought left a hole in her chest. He told her he loved her and she believed him. But that didn't tell her anything else about their future. As she tucked her phone back in her backpack, she couldn't help but think of the day she'd met sexy Vincent Hansen as she'd left a coffee date with a friend. He'd been leaning against the outside of the coffee shop, his muscular arms crossed over a very broad chest and wearing a bored expression on his dark, chiseled face. His leg had been in a cast and two crutches had leaned next to him as he waited for a friend who was getting some girl's phone number.

She'd felt such an immediate, almost visceral reaction to him, it had stunned her. When he'd turned those pale blue eyes on her, she knew he'd experienced something too. Because he'd given her a slow, almost wicked grin that promised all sorts of dirty, naughty things she'd only ever fantasized about. Her face had flamed and she was sure she'd imagined it until he came over and started flirting with her.

The man had had 'player' with a capital P written all over that handsome face and toothpaste commercial smile, but she'd been intrigued enough to give him her number. A week later they'd been sleeping together and exclusive. Something that was a first for him. Vincent had seemed almost embarrassed, even clueless, when he'd broached the subject of them being exclusive. When he'd admitted that he'd never had a girlfriend, just casual hookups, she'd realized the man basically had training wheels on when it came to relationships. Not that she was much better considering how infrequently she'd dated the past four years.

Now, four months later, she and Vincent were still together. He'd been in the Navy when they'd first met. As a SEAL at that. His injury had healed, but it was the type that wouldn't let him keep jumping out of planes and doing whatever else he did in the Navy that made him risk his life most of the time. So he'd decided to take an honorable discharge instead of remaining in the service. She was sad for him, but he was so positive about the future it was infectious. He'd been offered a job at a security company in Miami and he'd already taken it—she just wasn't sure when he was moving. It was close to his family and he was very tight with them.

Every time he spoke on the phone to his mother or one of his sisters, the love in his voice was evident. His tone and expression always softened and it made her heart melt. It was one of the things that had made her fall for him even harder. She had no family and she'd seen the way some of her friends treated their own with almost apathy. To her that was crazy; as long as they were good to you, family was forever and important. The people who would always have your back. So, the relocation for Vincent just made sense. Of course, she wasn't sure where she fit into his plans.

Things between them had been amazing. If he hadn't been laid up with a tibia fracture for the first couple months they'd been together they wouldn't have been able to spend so much time with each other. It wasn't that she was glad he'd been injured when they met, but she was glad they'd been able to spend all that time together because it had formed such a deep bond for them. Well, at least on her part.

He was possessive, dominating and just damn sexy. And he was all hers. Since they'd been together, she'd only had a taste of what life with him would be like and she'd loved every second of it. The whole Miami thing freaked her out though because he hadn't asked her to move with him. Now she was starting to wonder if maybe that wasn't part of his plan. The truth was, she would move anywhere in the world with that man. He just had to ask.

Shaking her head, she realized she probably looked like an idiot just sitting and staring off into space in the empty parking lot. The bookstore was closed, as were most of the shops along this quiet strip, and she had more important things to do.

As she started to turn her key in the ignition, something bright flashed out of the corner of her eye, drawing her attention.

Blinking, it took a moment for her to realize what she was seeing. The clothing boutique next door was on *fire*. Flames licked across the roof and up the outer walls, eating up everything in its way in seconds. As if the building was made of paper. Her friend Ginger had poured so much time, energy and love into that shop...

Jumping into action, she grabbed her phone from her backpack and dialed 9-1-1.

The operator's voice was crisp and clear. "9-1-1, what is the nature of your emergency?"

"My friend's shop is on fire!" Jordan quickly relayed the address and the carnage of what she was seeing. While talking, Jordan realized Ginger's truck was still in the parking lot. Ginger was the owner of the store and Jordan's friend.

She could still be inside. Or worse.

Terror gripped her as she realized what might be happening. For the past month a madman had been targeting various businesses across the San Diego area, burning buildings to the ground. It was always right after dusk and the places were always owned by women. All the owners had gone missing. Twenty-two in total. No one knew what had happened to them, but there was a lot of speculation.

There was no way Jordan could sit in her vehicle and just wait for the fire department and police. Against the female operator's protests, Jordan dropped her phone and pulled out the Taser Vincent had given her. She didn't know if she'd need it, but she wasn't taking any chances in case Ginger's store had been a target of the serial arsonist.

Hurrying from her Jeep, she didn't waste time to close the door behind her as she jumped out. Only an alleyway separated their stores, nothing more. Heart pounding out of control, she raced across the pavement, her sandals snapping loudly.

When she approached her friend's ten-year-old truck she nearly stumbled at the eerie, creaking sounds of the building imploding on itself from all that heat. Though she wanted to, she couldn't race into a crumbling building. It would be suicide. She just prayed Ginger hadn't been inside.

Maybe she was just down the street at one of the local coffee shops. There were three in this neighborhood alone and Ginger got her caffeine fix multiple times a day at one or all of them. When Jordan didn't see her friend in the truck, she started to head toward the next alleyway that separated the boutique and the vintage record store next to it.

She froze as she spotted a huge man with his back to her dragging something—someone!—out of the alley. Jordan couldn't make out everything, but she could see Ginger's bright red ballet slipper shoes dragging against the pavement. They were sparkly and ridiculous and she called them her Dorothy shoes.

Ducking behind the back of the truck, Jordan took a deep breath and forced herself to focus. The scent of the smoke from the fire filled the air and she felt frozen in fear. She clutched the Taser in her hand, knowing she had to act fast.

From all the news stories, when the women connected to the fires had disappeared, so had their vehicles. What if this guy planned to kidnap Ginger and drive away in her truck? She peeked around the back and saw how close the guy was. He was almost to the bed of the truck—and Jordan belatedly realized the tailgate was already down. Yeah, no doubt he was planning to dump Ginger's body in there.

Calling on strength she didn't know she had, she jumped from her hiding spot, aimed the Taser at the guy's back and pulled the trigger.

Chapter 1

Seven years later

Out of the corner of his eye, Vincent noticed the same four-door sedan he'd seen drive down his street slowly cruise by his house again. For the third time.

This time it stopped in front of a house two down from his and idled. He lived on a quiet, dead-end street and he recognized all the vehicles on sight. Even if one of his neighbors had bought a new car while he'd been out of town, there was no reason for the driver to be creeping around like they planned to do a drive-by. Not that he was actually worried about that. This was a middle class Miami neighborhood that rarely saw crime. But he believed in being vigilant.

Vincent kept his stride even as he walked from his neighbor's house to his. His fifty year old next-door neighbor had collected his mail for him while he'd been in Vegas at his friend Iris's wedding. He still had a couple more days off and he planned to spend it with his family. If he didn't go see his mom soon she'd chew his ass out and then he'd hear about it from his three sisters. Now that they all lived in the same city, he caught hell if he didn't see them on a regular basis. He might complain about them hassling him, but he loved them more than anything.

Right now he was going to find out who the hell was in that vehicle. Something about the way the person drove told him they weren't lost. Maybe he was being paranoid, but he always trusted his gut and he always looked out for his neighbors. Life could change in an instant—something he knew from personal experience—and he wasn't someone who sat idly by and did nothing if this was a potential criminal casing his neighborhood. He just wasn't wired that way. Probably his Navy training.

Once inside his house he dropped his mail on the small table in the foyer, then raced for the backdoor. The sun was setting, giving him enough shadows to blend in for what he planned. His backyard had a privacy fence so he climbed it into his neighbors' yard. Even if any of his neighbors saw him it was unlikely they'd be worried. He'd been nominated as unofficial leader of their neighborhood watch and he took his job seriously. Plus when he'd retrieved his mail his neighbor had mentioned a few petty break-ins a few blocks over while he'd been out of town.

Using the lengthening shadows, he scaled fences and jogged across backyards until he was six houses down. Adrenaline pumping, he hurried to his neighbors' front yard and scaled another privacy fence because it was locked. His feet hit the grass with a soft thump and a second later, a security flood light came on, illuminating the side of the house. He inwardly cursed even though he was the one who'd recommended everyone on the street get the lights. Pausing, he took a moment before he peered around the corner of the house.

From his angle he was still hidden from view of whoever was in that vehicle, which was good. Instead of using the well lit sidewalk, he quickly walked across his neighbors' front yards, avoiding kids' toys and other crap left out. Two dogs barked in the distance, then he heard the soft sound of Mr. Canning's automatic sprinkler going on like clockwork as he closed the distance.

Two yards to go. Then one.

The car still idled and even though the windows were tinted he could see the outline of a driver in the front seat. There was no one else in the vehicle and the person was small. Their head fit right against the headrest, but they were looking down at something in their hands.

Normally Vincent was armed, but hadn't felt it necessary now. Besides, with his training, he could take almost anyone out in hand-to-hand combat. He closed the last few feet to the car, sliding along the side until he reached the driver's door. He really hoped he was overreacting and this driver was just someone lost, but in his neighborhood, he never took chances.

He rapped his knuckles against the top of the car. Judging from the small size of the person, he guessed it was a woman. She jumped and dropped whatever had been in her hands.

Good.

He'd wanted to startle the driver, take her off guard and it worked.

A second later, the door opened and as the dome light flooded the interior and he saw *her* sitting there, he froze.

For a moment, it was as if time stood still. His surroundings, his neighbors' houses, the distant familiar sounds of the evening, just fell away in that moment. All he could do was stare as her head tilted up toward him and he found himself looking into familiar hazel eyes.

His chest constricted and he tried to drag in a breath, but it was as if an elephant was sitting on his chest.

Moving, breathing, thinking—impossible. His heart was a staccato beat against his ribs as he tried to control his breathing. He blinked once, sure this was a hallucination.

Or a fantasy he'd conjured up.

Nope, she was still there.

Her small hands were clasped tightly in her lap, her dark hair a sensual cascade falling over one shoulder as she stared right back.

His hands fell to his sides as he stared at Jordan Alvarado. The woman he'd loved more than anything. The woman who'd disappeared from his life seven years ago without a fucking word. The woman he'd never been able to get over. No matter how damn hard he tried. She was under his skin and in his heart, and nothing he'd done had worked her out of his system.

Her hazel eyes were wide as she watched him with a mix of nervousness and...lust. Yeah, that had always been there between them. The explosive attraction was like a living thing. Combustible and raw. That definitely hadn't changed. And he hated that he felt it too.

"Jordan." He hadn't realized he'd been about to speak until he heard his own raspy voice scraping out her name.

Her seatbelt was already off and he watched as she swallowed hard then took a tentative step out. She wrapped her arms around herself, her petite, compact body still as lush as he remembered. The halter-style dress she wore showed off all her curves and bronzed skin. Her dark hair had grown at least six inches since the last time he'd seen her. Back then she'd kept it shorter, so that it fell in a longer angle around her face and was shorter in the back. Now it was long, falling in soft waves. He wanted nothing more than to run his hands through it. "Vincent, I...you look really great," she said softly, too many emotions to define in her expression.

He couldn't help himself. He had a billion questions—like where the hell had she been for so long—but he was overcome with the need to taste her. To dominate and possess her. It had always been like that between them, but he'd convinced himself that the electricity wasn't real. That he'd built it up in his mind. People just didn't react that way to each other after so long but here she was standing in front of him and all he wanted to do was jump her. To take her hard and fast against the car, right out in the open for anyone to see.

Normally he was in absolute control of himself but before he'd realized he even intended to move, his lips were on hers and he was crushing her against the car.

Jordan moved against him like liquid sin, her body melting into his as if they were made for each other. Her fingers dug into his shoulders and one of her legs came up around him, her sandaled foot digging into his ass as she grinded against him.

He felt fevered with her so close, as if seven years hadn't passed. His hands skimmed down her sides until he reached around her body and grabbed her ass. He just barely restrained himself from gripping her too hard as he clutched her. The thin material of her dress told him she either had nothing on underneath or a thong he couldn't feel from this angle. Either option was hot as hell.

When she moaned into his mouth, his hips rolled against hers, his cock pulsing and pushing against the zipper of his pants. He wanted in her so bad he was consumed with the need.

"Mr. Hansen!"

Vincent jerked back at the sound of his name being called. Blinking, he stared down at Jordan for a moment as it slowly registered where he was and what he'd just done. What was wrong with him? He'd just acted like an animal. She looked dazed as she seemed to mentally shake herself. Her leg fell from around him and he turned in the direction of the familiar voice.

Vincent cleared his throat, actually embarrassed as he faced Mr. Baird, a seventy year old man who lived five houses down from him. His expression was sour, as always, as he stood on the sidewalk with his leashed dog that couldn't weigh more than eight pounds. "Sorry, Mr. Baird."

The man's lips just pursed as he shook his head and continued shuffling down the sidewalk, muttering under his breath about disgusting young people and their lack of common decency.

Vincent turned back to Jordan and forced himself under control. He couldn't just jump her like this—even if she was willing—before getting answers. For all he knew she was engaged or…married. The thought made his gut roil even though he had no claim on her. Not anymore. Maybe he never really had. "Keys," he said more forcefully than he'd intended.

Her swollen lips parted slightly as she looked at him in confusion. Yeah, she was still feeling the effects of that kiss too. "What?"

"Where are you car keys?"

"Still in the ignition."

"Good." He gently moved her out of the way and slid into the front seat. "My house, now. I'll park this in my driveway."

Obviously she knew which house was his because she was here. There was no way in hell it was a coincidence that she'd driven past his house three times and was sitting in his neighborhood. Without giving her a chance to respond, he shut the door. He had no clue what was going on, but he wasn't letting her behind the wheel. It was primitive and probably insane, but he didn't want to give her the chance to leave. Not until he found out where the hell she'd been and why she'd left him.

He'd spent so much damn time looking for her it was embarrassing. To have her show up at his place after so long rattled him more than he wanted to admit. She'd always done that to him though. Had from the moment he'd spotted her on that sidewalk back in San Diego.

After parking her car in his driveway he found her waiting on his front porch, her arms wrapped around her slim body as she watched him warily. He didn't like that look. Of course, he had a feeling he wasn't going to like whatever she had to tell him now. Someone didn't show up after seven years like this with good news.

Wordlessly he opened the door and motioned for her to walk inside. A single light above them illuminated the tanned glow of her bronzed skin. Even though she was clearly nervous she looked amazing. A little slimmer than he remembered but she still had great curves. He couldn't get the feel of her lush breasts pressing against his chest out of his head. All he wanted to do was strip off that dress and feast on her body.

But first… "I guess I should be fucking civilized and offer you something to drink but I want answers. Where have you been? Why'd you leave without a word?" He cursed himself that his voice shook, but it couldn't be helped. He'd loved her and she'd ripped his heart out.

She clasped her hands in front of her stomach and looked down at them. "Could we maybe sit?"

He wanted to say no, but he couldn't deny her anything. Not when she looked as if she was ready to burst into tears. Concern thrummed through him, but she was here and unharmed. It was clear she'd left him of her own free will all those years ago. He'd seen her empty apartment and talked to her former landlord.

Jordan had paid to break her contract and get out of her lease early and had hired movers to take care of all her things. It wasn't as if she'd been kidnapped. No, she'd left of her own damn free will.

Grunting, he flipped on lights as he strode down the hallway to his kitchen and leaned against one of the counters. The room was pristine since he rarely cooked and he hadn't been home for almost a week anyway. He motioned to the chairs tucked under the island.

Jordan pulled out a ladder back chair one of his sisters had made for him and perched on it. She nervously tapped her fingers against the granite topped island as she glanced around the kitchen. It was obvious she was curious about his place, but he wanted his damn answers.

"Talk, Jordan." He felt like he was about to explode.

Her gaze snapped back to his and he saw a myriad of regret and sadness. "I don't even know where to start so...God, this is so much harder than I thought it would be."

Hard? Like what he had gone through after she'd disappeared from his life without a word hadn't been fucking *hard*?

She shook her head, as if clearing her mind. "Do you remember Curtis Woods?"

The name sounded vaguely familiar but he shook his head, struggling for patience.

"Seven years ago he was the man responsible for all those fires in San Diego." Her voice was shaky, unsteady as she spoke and it rattled a memory loose.

"Yeah, I remember. All those women went missing after each fire." It had happened right around the time Vincent had gotten out of the Navy and had taken a job with Red Stone Security. But he hadn't moved to Miami yet because he'd been waiting for Jordan to graduate so he could propose. He'd wanted her to come with him and he'd been so sure she would.

Just proved what a fucking idiot he'd been.

"He burned down the clothing boutique next to that little bookstore I worked at. I didn't see him set the actual fire, but I caught him dragging the owner out after he'd set it. He'd drugged her and had planned to kill her—among other things—but he accidentally overdosed her in his hurry to escape the blaze. He didn't admit it until later, but the fire started too soon. I guess he got cocky and messed things up. Anyway, I saw the blaze and called the cops but when I saw him I couldn't just do nothing and let him escape. I… I used that Taser you gave me and disabled him. By the time the cops showed up it was a complete nightmare. The cops, the Feds and the Attorney General's office—everyone wanted to talk to me."

As she spoke, his gut clenched. He had a feeling he knew where she was headed but he remained silent, letting her speak. She was talking so fast he could tell she was just trying to get the words out and he wanted to hear everything.

"He pled not guilty even though he clearly was. As the only witness, they wanted to put me into WITSEC until the trial. At first I said no but he had a twin brother he was close with who they suspected was his accomplice. Eventually Woods admitted his brother helped him and he told the authorities where most of the bodies of those women were. He gave them twenty-one graves but held back one. Sick bastard," she muttered. "But before he confessed to everything, his attorneys dragged everything out for years. He was eventually convicted and a few months ago his brother was found dead behind a bar in Abilene, Texas. A week after that Woods killed himself in prison. So…I'm free again. I took my real name back and left the program. Vincent, I…I'm so sorry for leaving. I've missed you every single day. I…" She stopped talking, as if she'd run out of steam and watched him with a touch of fear in her eyes.

That just pissed him off. She should never be afraid of him, but he was so fucking angry he could barely see straight. "I remember when they caught that guy." He vaguely remembered the details of the news coverage because he'd been so busy getting his life squared away to move. "I also remember that you didn't fucking *disappear* for days after he was arrested. You know why I remember? Because we fucked so much I could barely walk." It had been such an intense time in their relationship, like she'd been branding him as her own. Now he realized it was because she'd planned to leave. "I *loved* you, Jordan." She was the only woman he'd ever loved, something she'd known. He'd stumbled over telling her that first time, had felt like an idiot, but once he'd told her, it had been freeing.

"You could have asked me to join WITSEC with you." God, he would have too. In a heartbeat. But he didn't say that because she clearly hadn't cared enough about him to ask. She hadn't felt the same way he had.

Jordan let out a harsh, scraping laugh that sounded hollow. "Vincent, I wanted to so badly but… I couldn't put you in that position. You would have had to leave your family and life forever. At the time I had no clue if Woods' brother would ever be caught or found. I planned to be in WITSEC forever and I couldn't make you leave your family like that. You wouldn't have been able to work in the field you chose and you'd have had to leave *everyone* behind. Your mother, your sisters, all your friends in the Navy. Those men are like your brothers. How the hell could I do that to you? To the man I loved?"

He scrubbed a hand over his face and forced himself to stay where he was when he wanted to stalk across the kitchen and shake some sense into her. "So you made the decision for me? You just decided I didn't love you enough to go with you?"

"No! It wasn't like that. We'd only been together four months and you hadn't even mentioned me moving to Miami with you. It wasn't fair of me to ask you something so life changing. I knew the type of man you were and I was worried you'd feel obligated or something. I didn't want to put you in a position where you *had* to make that choice. If you'd said yes, eventually you would have either resented me or just died inside. No way was I tearing your life apart like that." Tears shimmered in her hazel eyes, but he hardened himself against the sight.

Grabbing her car keys out of his pocket he strode toward her and slammed them on the island. "Get the fuck out of my house."

She flinched at his words. "Vincent, I'm sorry. So sorry you can't even know. You've never left my mind. God, I've missed you so much and I know I don't deserve your forgiveness, but I'm asking for it. I've been working up the courage to see you for the past two months and—"

"Get. Out. Now." He barely managed to get the words out before he turned his back on her and took a deep breath.

"Vincent..." Her voice cracked and he felt the light brush of her fingertips on his back, but he stepped away and stalked out his backdoor into the humid summer night.

Fuck, fuck, *fuck*. He could barely see or think straight. Seven fucking years without a word and she thought she could just walk back into his life and say she was sorry.

Living without her had been hell. He didn't know how to handle this, how to handle having her abruptly show up again. She wanted his forgiveness but what else did she want from him? He felt like a fucking idiot still desiring her. How could she have left like that without telling him? He'd bought her a ring, had been ready to propose. Hell, he still had the thing in his safe. For some reason he'd never been able to force himself to sell it. Taking a deep breath, some of his anger dissipated. No matter how angry he was, he couldn't let things end like this. He couldn't just kick her out. Not when he still needed answers.

Even though he had no clue what to say to her, he headed back inside and found the kitchen empty. The subtle scent of her familiar perfume lingered in the air. Light vanilla and something that was all Jordan wrapped around him as he raced back through the house. He didn't have her phone number or any clue where she was staying. He wanted to kick his own ass when he jerked open the door and saw the taillights of her car turning at the end of his street.

Cursing at himself he pulled his cell phone out and called the one person he knew who would be able to help quicker than anyone; Lizzy Caldwell. The woman might have had a baby two months ago but she was a computer genius and Vincent knew she was itching to get back to work. Now that Jordan had reclaimed her own name, Lizzy would have no problem tracking her down.

Whatever hell Jordan had put him through, Vincent intended to finish this one way or another.

Chapter 2

Vincent stood in the lobby of Porter and Lizzy's high rise condo building, trying to control his racing heart. It was no use. The longer it took to see Jordan again, the more stressed he got. What the fuck had he been thinking, kicking her out like that? He hadn't been thinking at all. He'd just been so pissed at everything. All the years she'd been gone, the fact that she hadn't trusted him enough to make the decision about their future for himself.

And…he hated that she'd had to go through so much by herself. Starting over, leaving everything she'd known, testifying against a monster—it had taken a lot of strength to do that even if she should have told him the truth from the start.

"You can go up." The man behind the security desk finally spoke as he placed the cordless phone back on its base on the desk.

"Thanks," Vincent murmured.

Porter's place had excellent security and all the residents had to use a biometric scanner to access the elevators—unless a security member overrode the system. And those guys were armed to the teeth. Normally Vincent wouldn't bother any of his coworkers with something like this, but he needed help, and Lizzy and Porter were more than just co-workers. So he swallowed his pride because finding Jordan was worth it. He just couldn't let her walk out of his life again.

The ride up to his friends' place was quick. Too damn quick. He felt so exposed knowing he'd have to admit why he wanted Lizzy's help. The elevator opened up into an airy, open entryway. There was only one door ahead of him and before he'd taken two steps it opened.

Porter strode out, looking exhausted—likely from being a new parent—but he also looked worried. "Everything okay? We didn't realize our phones were even off until security buzzed us."

Another reason Vincent felt like a jackass showing up at their place unannounced. They could have been catching up on sleep. "Yeah, everything's fine. I, uh, I would never ask this unless it was important. I need Lizzy's expertise finding someone." He rubbed the back of his neck.

"This isn't work related." Not a question.

Vincent shook his head. "It's...personal."

Porter's blue eyes widened. "Holy shit, is this about a woman?"

Vincent's jaw clenched, but he didn't respond.

To his surprise, Porter grinned, his smile wide and almost mocking. For a man who rarely smiled except at his wife, the action took Vincent off guard. It also pissed him off. "This is funny to you?"

Porter shrugged. "It's a little funny. Come on. We just put the little guy to sleep. Probably won't stay down long but you have good timing."

Moments later he found Lizzy in the kitchen sitting at the counter with her laptop and a bottle of water. Wearing one of Porter's old Marine T-shirts and pajama pants that were also likely her husband's, she glanced up when she saw him and the same concern he'd witnessed on Porter's face was etched on her pretty features. "Vincent, is—"

He nodded, cutting her off. "I'm good, I just need a huge favor and only you can do it. I swear I wouldn't have bugged you guys, especially with the new baby, but I didn't know who else to ask." And he wouldn't have had to come to his friends if he hadn't kicked Jordan out of his house. He shoved that thought down as he tried to push away the memory of her tears. Right now he wanted to kick his own ass.

He should have stayed and hashed things out. And found out exactly what she wanted from him other than forgiveness. Because he wasn't sure he could let her walk away again. That thought pissed him off more than anything. It was just a reminder of how much power the petite woman wielded over him.

Lizzy's dark eyes lit up. "I've just been catching up on work emails so a chance to do something fun... Will any of this be illegal?" She sounded practically gleeful as she asked.

Vincent shrugged and despite his dark mood, he grinned. "I need to track a woman down by any means necessary. Tracking her credit cards, whatever it takes."

Lizzy started to speak, but the sound of Maddox wailing made them all pause. "I thought he was down for good this time," she murmured, exhaustion creeping into her gaze.

When she started to get up and Porter moved into action with her, Vincent shook his head as he pulled out the envelope that contained everything he knew about Jordan and laid it on the counter. Having worked with Lizzy before many times, he'd known what kind of questions she'd have so he was prepared. "Unless he's hungry I can take care of him and give you guys a break."

Porter and Lizzy looked at each other, both unsure.

Vincent had been over a few times since the birth so it wasn't as if he was a complete stranger to their baby. Plus, he had more than his fair share of experience with his two married sisters' kids. "My sisters call me the baby whisperer. Trust me." Without waiting for a response he headed for Maddox's room. Sure enough, the moment he picked up the tiny bundle of flailing fists and feet, the baby quieted down, giggling softly. Babies just liked to be held and made to feel secure most of the time. One of his sisters had told him it was because it reminded them of being in the womb.

Sitting in the rocking chair in the corner of the room, Vincent rocked back and forth in a steady rhythm, holding Maddox close to his chest. He had no clue what it was but babies just loved him. And he really loved them too. They smelled good most of the time and had such open, adorable expressions. Right now, he could sure use the distraction.

At one point Porter popped his head in the room and gave him an incredulous look, but just as quickly backed out again. Vincent wasn't sure how much time had passed because he started to doze too, but eventually Lizzy walked in looking very proud of herself.

Smiling at her sleeping baby, she gently took him from Vincent's arms. "I think I found your girl."

* * * * *

Jordan wrapped her beach towel tighter around her waist before gathering up everything she'd brought to the pool and dumping it in her red and white striped beach bag. Her worn paperback book, phone and sunscreen were all she needed today. After seven years of living in a state of fear and feeling like a giant liar to everyone she became friends with, she finally felt free. If a little lost.

And a little heartbroken. Not that she had anyone to blame but herself. Maybe she should have told Vincent the truth all those years ago, but she'd just loved him so damn much she hadn't been willing to shred his life apart. The thought of pushing him into a situation against his will like that had been too much to bear. She thought she'd been ready to give him up too. Until the reality of her new life had set in, but by then it had been too late.

As she headed for the stone stairs that led to the condo where she was staying, she rubbed the back of her neck and shoved those thoughts away. Seeing him two days ago had seriously messed with her mind.

She wasn't sure what she'd hoped to gain from seeing him. Forgiveness, for sure. Also, a little closure. She should have expected his anger, but for some reason she hadn't been prepared for the depth of it. After months of working up the courage to go see him, she still hadn't been ready to face him when he'd taken the decision out of her hands. She'd been so startled when he'd come up on her car like that she'd just opened the door without a thought.

Then when he'd kissed her… It had been like no time had passed between them. She swore the man had gotten even sexier.

The US Marshal who had been her handler had given Jordan all the information she'd requested on Vincent's current whereabouts when she'd left the program, including a recent picture of him. Jordan wasn't sure if it was even legal, but her handler had said she wanted to do it as a favor, so Jordan had taken all the information on Vincent and devoured it.

The photo hadn't done him justice. It had been one of those employee ones, like people took for passports.

Seeing him—and feeling him—up close and in person was like being doused in all that sexuality he exuded.

Tall, dark and handsome. That was Vincent. When he smiled, that bit of wicked charm glinted in his eyes, guaranteed to melt any woman with a pulse. And those eyes. A pale blue that had made her heart skip a beat the first time she'd seen him. She hated that she still reacted so much to him. Time and space should have dulled her response, but it seemed stronger now.

Sighing, she slid the key into the lock of the condo. She needed to get her head on straight and figure out what the hell she wanted to do with the rest of her life, not focus on things she couldn't change. Her friend Barbara, who she'd met while in WITSEC, had given Jordan free use of her condo in Key West for as long as she wanted this summer. She'd been worried about all her friends' reactions when she'd left the program and they learned the truth about her. But everyone had been great, even if it had been hard for them to get used to calling her by her real name.

The name Jordan had never wanted to part with in the first place. It had been her mother's name and pretty much the only thing Jordan had gotten from the woman who died giving birth to her. She'd been so happy to reclaim it even if it meant starting over again.

The cool air from the condo rushed over her as she stepped inside and shut the door. It was a sharp contrast from the humidity outside. Even though her bikini was almost dry after her last swim in the pool, her nipples beaded against the cloth triangles. The July heat here was brutal but she loved the sun and sand.

Stripping off her towel, she tossed it into the small laundry room as she made her way down the tiled hallway. As she stepped into the open area where the living room and kitchen joined, she froze.

With his back to her, Vincent stood staring out the

sliding glass doors that led to the small balcony. The pale green and yellow ceiling-to-floor length curtains had been pulled back, letting the afternoon sunlight spill in. His hands were shoved in his pockets and he was dressed casually in cargo shorts and a fitted T-shirt that showed off all his muscles.

She swallowed hard, her gaze traveling over his back, his very tight ass and—wait a minute. "What the hell are you doing here?" She blinked, making sure she hadn't imagined him and sure enough, he was still standing there.

He turned to face her, his eyes piercing as they took in her appearance. Wearing just her bikini, she felt vulnerable and exposed so she held her small beach bag up against her chest and looked at him with raised eyebrows. "Well?" After the way he'd kicked her out she'd been certain she'd never see him again.

"Your security here is shit," he finally said, as if he had every right in the world to be standing in front of her without invitation.

Not that she actually minded him standing there. She felt as if she was starving for just the sight of him as she devoured him with her eyes. Maybe she should be embarrassed about staring, but it was hard to stop herself.

"Don't look at me like that," he finally growled.

"Or what?"

"You really want to push me after it took two days— and seven fucking years—to find you again?" He took a step forward, looking like a sleek panther stalking his prey.

Jordan stood her ground even though her first instinct was to retreat. "Two days ago you told me to leave." Even though she hadn't wanted to, she also hadn't wanted to break down into a crying mess in front of him. Because that's what she'd done as soon as she'd left his house. Then she'd gone back to her hotel, packed all her stuff and headed to Key West.

"I did, but that was a mistake." He took another step with sleek animal-like grace.

Damn, she'd forgotten that he could move like that. It made her body flare to life despite the order she gave herself to stay unaffected by him. Now the way her nipples beaded against the soft fabric of her skimpy suit had nothing to do with the air conditioning. Yeah, her body so wasn't listening right now. It wanted what Vincent could give her. Raw, amazing orgasms. One after the other. "Mistake?" she whispered.

Nodding, he covered the short distance between them until she had no choice but to push the swivel wicker chairs along the counter out of the way as he backed her up against it. He was a lot taller than her so she had to look up to meet his gaze. She saw lust and anger there. Lots of anger.

When he didn't answer, she continued. "What do you want from me?"

His jaw tightened then and he shook his head, confusion filtering into his expression. "I...don't know. I'm so fucking pissed, Jordan."

Her throat tightened at those words. Maybe he was here to get his own closure, to rant at her until he felt better. She didn't know. Hell, she probably deserved it.

"But I'm also relieved to find out you're okay. And I shouldn't care, but I do. A lot." He plucked her bag from her hands and set it on one of the chairs.

Now there were no barriers between them. Unsure what to say, she just watched him, trapped by his gaze as he leaned down so that their faces were inches apart. He caged her in with his big arms, placing his hands on the counter on either side of her. Out of the corner of her eyes she could see his muscles flexing and she fought a shiver. She should not be getting turned on right now but her body was a traitorous bitch.

"Who's the guy in all the pictures?" he finally said, more than a touch of anger in his voice.

It took a moment for his words to register. "What?" What was he talking about?

"The photos all over this condo. Who is he?" Okay now he sounded jealous.

That surprised her. But she also wasn't afraid to admit she liked it. Her handler had told her that Vincent wasn't dating anyone, but Jordan hadn't expected any kind of entanglement with him anyway. She'd just wanted his forgiveness. Of course she hadn't expected the scorching attraction between them to still be there, burning out of control. "My friend Barbara's son. I've never met him, but she owns this place and she's letting me stay here. And…I'm pretty sure there are only a couple pictures of him."

The tension in his shoulders loosened, but he didn't move from his spot, completely invading her personal space. His familiar spicy, masculine scent surrounded her, making her feel almost lightheaded. She hated that she liked it so much, that she wanted to lean in and rub her breasts against him like a freaking cat in heat. Clearly she had issues.

"Are you seeing anyone?" he asked.

"No, are you?" Please let him say no. Her handler had told her that he wasn't, but her information might have been wrong or outdated. After the way he'd kissed her she doubted he was because Vincent wasn't a cheater. Still, she had to know.

"You think I would have kissed you if I was?" Now there was a definite rumble of anger in his voice.

"No."

"Is anyone else staying here with you?"

With his observation skills he had probably already guessed she was alone, but she shook her head. "No, why?"

"Because I don't want any interruptions." Taking her by surprise, he grasped onto her hips, his big palms gripping her firmly as he placed her on the low counter.

Like this, they were much closer in height. Before she realized his intentions, he threaded his fingers through her hair, pulling her head close as he barely skated his lips over hers, the action soft and sweet.

Her eyes drifted shut as he wrapped his other arm around her waist, pulling her close so that she had to widen her thighs and wrap her legs around him. She'd been fantasizing about this for so long it almost didn't seem real. In fact, she wondered if she was still down by the pool, dozing under the afternoon sun. Or maybe she was having heat stroke and hallucinating. No matter what, she didn't care. She wanted this. Wanted him so bad her body trembled.

The other day against her car she'd felt almost consumed with the need to jump him when he'd kissed her, but this was different. It was sweeter. But… she pulled back slightly, pleased that his breathing was just as erratic as hers. She didn't want to be the only one affected.

"What are you doing? You just show up without telling me how you even found me and… We need to talk before we do anything we'll regret." Okay, she probably wouldn't regret anything but she still wanted to talk to him. She didn't want fast and furious sex between them and while she didn't think he was jerk enough to fuck her out of some sense of revenge, she was feeling really raw and insecure. Maybe that *was* what he wanted.

"We're going to talk but first I'm going to taste you." His voice was a low, sensual rumble she felt all the way to her toes.

Taste her? He couldn't mean what she thought he did. As his mouth descended on hers once again, his kisses teasing and light, his hands skimmed down her sides until they grasped her bikini bottom and started tugging it down. Yep, he definitely meant what she thought. Her heart raced as her lower abdomen clenched and she couldn't stop the flood of heat that filled between her legs. Just the thought of him touching her got her wet.

Jordan briefly wondered if she should stop him. Talking some things out was the smart thing to do. Not getting naked. She didn't care about smart though. Instead, she lifted her hips and let him pull the bottom completely off.

Her skin was warm from being in the sun the past couple hours, but when his large hand cupped her mound, he lit her on fire. Slowly, he dragged a finger along the length of her slit, not even close to penetrating. She was already slick with want from their kisses, but to actually have Vincent touching her, teasing her, after so long, it was surreal.

He'd never been far from her thoughts. So many times she'd questioned her decision to leave until she thought she'd go mad. Now… she could barely think straight as he tentatively slid a finger into her tight sheath. She clenched around him, need building in her as she remembered what his hard length felt like, not just his finger. He'd always kept her on her toes. She'd never known whether he'd be rough and hot or sweet and gentle between the sheets. And she'd never cared because any time Vincent was inside her had been pure heaven. Just like she knew it would be now.

Her back arched, her covered breasts rubbing against his hard chest and without thinking, she reached behind her back and untied her top. It slackened, and before she had a chance to tug the tie around her neck, he plucked it free with his other hand.

"I've missed you," he murmured as he began

peppering kisses along her jaw, the soft action mirroring the slow, steady strokes of his finger.

Oh, God. Her entire body hummed with anticipation. She didn't want slow, but she wasn't going to push him. He was teasing her, working her up and she knew the payoff would be worth it. Vincent had never disappointed her. "I've missed you too." So much she ached over it.

When he reached her earlobe, he tugged it between his teeth, pressing down hard, the little bite of pleasure/pain shooting through her. Her fingers dug into his shoulders as she tried to steady herself, but she knew it was useless. He already had her off balance. Just by being in the same room as her, the sexy man knocked her world off kilter.

As he moved lower with his mouth, he flicked his tongue along her ear, then the column of her neck and followed up each time with gentle nips from his teeth. His movements were slow, designed to drive her crazy.

She wanted to touch him everywhere, to get him worked up as much as he was getting her. Sliding her hand down his chest, she reveled in the feel of all his strength. When she slid her hand over his covered cock and lightly squeezed, his big body shuddered.

"You're so tight, sweetheart," he murmured as he slid another finger inside her.

Yeah, there was a reason for that. "I haven't..." She trailed off, not wanting to go down that path as her inner walls molded to him, clenching around him and wanting so much more than just his fingers. She just wanted to feel, for them both to experience pleasure. He was right, they would talk later. Hopefully much later. After she'd kissed every inch of his delicious body and he'd done the same to hers.

His fingers were still inside her as he lifted his head. She couldn't define the look in his gaze as he watched her. Lust swelled beneath the surface but there was something else she didn't recognize. Oh crap, was he stopping? He wasn't pulling out, but he wasn't moving inside her either. She gently squeezed his cock again, taking pleasure when he trembled.

But he still didn't continue what he was doing. Instead, he pulled his fingers out of her completely and gripped her hips, his hands flexing against her bare flesh. "You haven't what?"

"Huh?" Why was he talking? She needed release, craved it so much she could almost taste it.

His blue eyes were steady on hers. "What were you going to say?"

Ugh, was he going to make her say it? She wanted to kick herself. Sometimes her mouth got away from her but she'd caught herself. "Now you want to talk?"

"Jordan." There was a warning note in his voice. One that made her nipples tingle in awareness.

"I haven't been with anyone in a long time." Since him. But she'd tried dating, hoping she'd find that crazy spark with someone else. At least enough of a spark to incite that sexual hunger she'd only ever had with Vincent. Unfortunately it had never happened and she hadn't been willing to settle for less than what she'd had with him. She just wasn't hardwired that way.

"How long?" His fingers clenched again.

Anger flared in her at the question. "Vincent, that's—"

"How. Long." There he went again with that demanding voice that sent a shiver of need down her spine.

She used to love it when he ordered her around in the bedroom. He was so forceful and dominating and everything about him had made her melt. Almost against her will she answered. "Since you."

At her words, anger flared in his eyes, the darkness

lighting up his pale gaze as he turned away from her. "No. Fuck *no*. Don't tell me that," he growled, anger burning in each word.

Suddenly chilled, she wrapped her arms around herself. Being naked like this with him still clothed and angry, she felt emotionally vulnerable. "Well, it's true."

He scrubbed a hand over his head but didn't turn around. "I'm taking you to dinner tonight. I'll pick you up at six." Then he left in a few long strides, the front door slamming behind him before she had a chance to even figure out what the hell had gone wrong.

Chapter 3

That bitch was going to pay. Jordan Alvarado thought she could get away with what she'd done, but she was about to learn the hard way what real suffering meant. Putting a tracker on her phone had been tricky, but after stealing it then cloning it before slipping it back into her purse, tailing Jordan to Key West had been relatively easy.

The man who'd shown up at her condo today was interesting. He was the same one she'd gone to see in Miami. So he obviously meant something to Jordan. And that was something that could be used against her.

Jordan was responsible for Curtis's death, whether indirectly or not, so making her pay was necessary. Curtis had been the best brother in the world. He'd been everything.

The fact that hurting Jordan's friend would be fun didn't matter. She would suffer over losing him, then die. Figuring out exactly who her visitor was first though, was important.

After he left her condo, the tall man made his way

through the city until he finally stopped around upper Duval Street. There was a private turnoff that was easy to miss because of the security gate. His car slowed then idled as a gate rolled back to reveal a courtyard and small cottage. The place might be small but with private, off street parking in this part of town—that place would be a pretty penny. And it didn't look like a rental.

So either the unknown male was wealthy or he had friends who were. Which meant he likely did well for himself, too, because rich people didn't hang out with poor people. His place in Miami had been very nice and the security sticker sign on one of his windows had indicated his system was state of the art. Not the standard companies most people went with.

He hadn't been very interesting until now, but if getting to Jordan through him was possible, that's the way it would be. Unfortunately the man had looked armed and definitely dangerous. A slight bulge under the back of his T-shirt had been visible when he'd been leaving the condo where Jordan was staying.

Likely a gun.

He could be a cop or law enforcement, especially with the easy way he'd broken into her place without a key. Seeing the guy in action and the way he handled himself would reveal more about who he was. And what his weakness was. Everyone had one.

At that thought, a plan started to form.

* * * * *

Vincent ordered himself to keep his shit together as he knocked on Jordan's door. Six was early for dinner, but he wanted to see her. Hell, he hadn't wanted to leave at all. When he'd arrived at her place earlier, he'd realized how bad her security was—translation, non-existent. The woman should be looking after herself better. Especially after she'd been in WITSEC. He didn't care that she'd left the program and was supposedly out of jeopardy. She'd put a dangerous criminal behind bars.

He'd wanted to prove a point to her about how easy it would be for someone to break in, but then he'd seen her in that barely-there bikini and his brain had completely short-circuited.

Tan and fit with just the right amount of curves, she had the ability to make any sane man forget his own name. Not touching her, not tasting her, hadn't been an option. Then when she'd admitted she hadn't been with anyone since him…it had cracked his heart wide open.

He might have thought he'd come to Key West to get closure on what they'd had, but this new knowledge changed everything and he couldn't deny it. While he hated that she had taken away his choice to go with her, she wasn't some cold hearted woman who'd just left him with no regard for what they'd shared. Because for years he'd tried to tell himself she was, even when deep down he'd *known* something had happened to make her run. He just hadn't imagined she'd entered WITSEC.

She'd made a sacrifice that most people wouldn't have. And it made him respect her more. It also brought up all those feelings he'd been trying so hard to keep buried the last seven years. For a while he'd tried to lose himself in other women. It hadn't worked. If anything, it had made him feel even more hollow. After having the real thing with Jordan, every other experience had left him wanting and made him hate himself just a little. Sure, everyone at work thought he was a player. He had been.

Not the past year though. He'd gotten tired of pasting on a big smile and looking for what he'd had with Jordan only to find it paled in comparison and regretting the whole thing the next morning. So many of his friends had started settling down with the real deal. Porter,

Travis, and Kell—they'd all gotten hitched and were obnoxiously happy.

He wanted that too. When he'd been in the Teams, he'd always secretly envied the married guys. Well, the ones who were actually faithful to their wives. They always had someone to come home to. And wives who could tough out long separations like that—what sane man wouldn't want a woman like that. But he wasn't looking to just settle. Jordan had ruined him for any other woman and he hadn't realized it until it was too late.

The door opened and all those thoughts—and everything else around him—disappeared as he found Jordan standing there. She wore a blue and white halter style dress that fell to her ankles. It hugged her breasts and hips perfectly, reminding him of what he'd been touching only hours ago. Her skin practically glowed with the soft tan.

Somehow he forced his gaze to remain on hers instead of devouring her body with his eyes. "You look beautiful."

She seemed almost surprised by the compliment, but her cheeks tinged pink. "Thanks," she murmured. "You look pretty good yourself."

God, he used to love getting her to blush. Seeing her do it now sent a jolt of need straight to his cock. *Just great.* He ordered his body under control. Tonight he wanted to talk to her, to get to know her again before he jumped on her as he'd done a few hours ago.

Not that getting naked with her wasn't a priority, because it definitely was. He just didn't want to screw things up. The attraction between them was still potent, but he wanted more than sex between them. He wanted what they'd had before.

Something real.

They stood there for a long moment, just staring at

each other and in her gaze he saw what he imagined was mirrored in his. Hunger and need. God, he felt as if he'd been starving for years and now he simply couldn't stop looking at her. He wanted to memorize every inch of her face, her body, the way she bit her full bottom lip when she was nervous or turned on.

Like she was doing now.

Stop staring. Stop fantasizing. Yeah, his internal commands weren't working so well. "You hungry?" he managed to rasp out, proud of himself for those two words.

At his question, her hazel eyes flared with need. But then she slightly shook her head, as if she realized he was talking about food. Which he was, sort of. "Yeah." Her voice was as strained as his.

She stepped outside and pulled the door shut behind her. After locking it, she turned to face him again.

He couldn't help himself. Screw control. He had none. Leaning forward, he brushed his lips over hers and felt some primal part of him calm. She shuddered, softly kissing him back as her fingers barely grazed his chest. He could feel her holding back, too, as if she was afraid to clutch him too tightly.

Because if she did, they both knew what would happen. They wouldn't make it to dinner or possibly off this front stoop.

Somehow he forced himself to step back. Her eyes were bright and her cheeks were flushed with arousal. Yeah, he understood that all too well. Swallowing hard, he took her hand and linked his fingers through hers.

Again, she seemed surprised by him, but he couldn't help it. Staying away from her, finding closure…fuck it. He couldn't help but wonder if she was going to rip his heart out again, but he was going to find out. Maybe he was a masochist.

"So where are we going?" she asked as they walked

down the stone steps of the condo complex.

He shrugged. "I figured we could walk down Duval and stop wherever we wanted. Unless you had somewhere specific you wanted to go?"

"As long as we get seafood I'm happy. After living in the desert for so long, I want fresh seafood." He could hear the smile in her voice without even looking at her.

As they reached the bottom step he glanced around the parking lot, looking for any threat. Doing that was just ingrained in him, but as he'd headed up to Jordan's place he'd had the sensation of being watched. Having been in the crosshairs of a sniper scope more than once, he knew when someone was watching him. It could have been anything though. Still...

"What's wrong?" Jordan's strained voice pulled him out of his thoughts.

Seeing concern on her face jolted him, made a protective need surge through him full force. He wrapped his arm around her shoulders and pulled her tight. Thankfully she didn't resist, just slid her arm around his waist and snuggled up next to him.

"Nothing's wrong. Just being vigilant." No need to get her worried after she'd lived in fear for seven fucking years. Especially since he wasn't sure anything was wrong. Still, that feeling persisted at the back of his head.

She instantly relaxed against him, her body melding to his as they headed across the parking lot to the sidewalk. Her fresh vanilla scent teased him, reminding him of how many times he'd woken up with his face buried against her neck. Even in his sleep he'd wanted her surrounding him. "I'm glad you're like that. I feel like I've been looking over my shoulder for seven years—is it okay that I talk about this stuff?" she abruptly asked.

"I want to know everything about where you've

been." And he did.

"Same here. I want to know about your job, your family, everything." She seemed a little nervous as she said the last word, but he couldn't figure out why.

As they headed down the small side street that would take them to the main road where all the restaurants, bars and clubs were, he kept his body on the street side.

"And I'll tell you, but you're up first," he said.

"Well, after the first year of bouncing around to different temporary safe houses, I was placed in New Mexico. It was really hard at first. I…didn't adjust well. But eventually I got a job teaching."

"They let you teach?" He didn't know everything about the WITSEC program, but he knew a little. And after Jordan had come to see him a couple days ago he'd tried to research as much as he could. From what he understood, they didn't always let their entrants stay in the same field they'd been in because it made them easier to track. Especially if their field of expertise was narrow.

"Yeah. I didn't at first, but I was finally allowed to. There are so many schools, public and private, it would be almost impossible to track me down that way. Plus I was vigilant about no photos of me ever being posted on the school website. I didn't even take one with the volleyball team I coached. The first year they didn't seem to understand, but my girls were amazing. I coached them from the time they were freshmen and by their senior year it was sort of a joke that the coach wouldn't ever pose for social media photos." The joy on her face when she talked about her team was vivid. And he was so fucking glad she'd eventually settled in somewhere. He still hated that she'd left without telling him, but the thought of her being miserable carved him up inside.

"So you taught the junior and varsity team?" She'd

loved playing in college. She was too short to ever make a serious team, but she'd played at the beach anytime she could. And she'd looked damn sexy playing in her two-piece suits. Those images were seared into his brain forever.

"Yeah, the first two years it was the freshmen and sophomores. The varsity coach was retiring so it was like kismet. I just moved up with them and after they all graduated, I stayed with the varsity team. I'd already started coaching the incoming juniors anyway and I just love that age. Everything in life is so fresh and dramatic for them. It was fun watching so many wonderful young women heading off into the world, ready to take anything on."

He tightened his grip on her shoulders as they sidestepped a street entertainer playing a guitar on the sidewalk. "You miss them."

"Yeah. I've stayed in touch with those that I was close with. It's been pretty freeing to be able to be honest with them now that they know my real name. But enough about me, how is it working for Red Stone? I remember how excited you were to get an offer from them. Is it what you hoped?"

He stopped at a small restaurant that had an outside patio and glanced at the glassed-in menu on the outside of the hostess stand. "I'll tell you everything, but first, how does this place look?"

"Coconut shrimp, pan-grilled barbeque shrimp, lobster, seared tuna…I think I'm in heaven."

The joy in her voice and on her face was so open, so real, it was a punch to his senses. He couldn't believe he'd lived so long without her. With that thought, it brought up the reminder that she'd left him. He didn't want it to make him angry, but it did.

"What?" Her smile fell and he could feel her start to emotionally pull away from him even before she tried to step out of his embrace.

Tried. Because he wouldn't let her. It was like he physically couldn't. Vincent tightened his grip and kissed the top of her head. "Let's grab a table on the patio." The sign said to seat themselves so he snagged two menus before they headed over.

He had to decide if he could let his own anger go before he took things further between them. He knew that. Figuring out how to do it was the tough part.

Chapter 4

Jordan couldn't get over the fact that Vincent was sitting across from her. Over dinner they'd caught up on the last seven years. Of course it wasn't enough, and she still wanted to know a lot more, but she loved hearing about his life. And she was glad he wasn't dating someone at the moment. The thought of him with other women...no, she wasn't even going there. It hurt too much.

"You ready?" he asked as he set the black bill pad on the table.

She'd tried to pay but he'd been almost insulted as he'd snatched the pad from their server. Even though she wished they could sit there all night and talk, she nodded. The night had to end sometime. She nodded and stood. "Yeah."

"Maybe we can grab gelato on the way back. I remember how much you love it," he murmured against her ear as he tugged her close to his side, his voice completely wicked.

At those words, her entire body went molten hot. Damn him and his memory. And damn him for turning her on with just a few words. Because she had no doubt that he knew exactly what he was doing. More than once she'd let him eat it off her body—and she'd done the same to him. "You have a very good memory," she muttered, nudging him with her elbow.

He just wrapped his muscular arm around her shoulders and pulled her close once again. She'd missed that closeness, his warmth, and the way he always made her feel safe and protected. Vincent had never had a problem with displaying affection.

Now that the sun had set, people were out in full party mode. It didn't matter that it was a Tuesday night; it was summer and everyone was here to let loose. The island music, the sound of laughter, talking and people just having a good time was infectious and relaxing. For the first time in a while she felt as if she could truly let her guard down. Well, almost. She wasn't letting the guard around her heart totally down, but she liked being able to be herself. Especially with Vincent.

Lord, he was sexy tonight. Wearing simple cargo shorts and a T-shirt with some surf brand logo on the front, he looked good enough to eat. The shirt molded to all his muscles, showing off every sexy line and striation. Even his freaking calves were toned, delicious and so sexy she wanted to lick them. Calves should *not* be sexy. It didn't matter that he wasn't a SEAL anymore, the man was *built*. And pretty much every female—and quite a few men—had been checking him out all during their dinner. Not that she really cared since he hadn't even seemed to notice. Of course he probably had, but he hadn't let on.

At the beginning of the meal he'd seemed to almost pull back from her emotionally, but he didn't have eyes for anyone else as they'd talked and ate. Not that he ever had when they'd been together. He might have been a player before her, but with her, he'd been devoted. She missed that more than she'd thought possible. She just hated the hot and cold vibe she was getting from him.

"I remember all the dirty stuff." His voice was teasing and light as they strolled down the sidewalk.

She just bet he did because she did too. In explicit detail. "So...do you want to do anything else tonight?" Because she really didn't want to spend the night alone at the condo. She'd come here to hibernate, to figure stuff out, but now that Vincent was in town she wanted to soak up every second she could with him.

He would break her heart. She knew that. Hell, she figured she deserved it. But she didn't care. Not after living without him for so long.

"I can think of a lot of things I'd like to do," he murmured, the words deep and raspy. The meaning behind them was clear too.

And didn't that just make her nipples tighten almost painfully. She was wearing a thin bandeau bra under her halter dress and knew her reaction must be blatant. She risked a quick glance up at him, but he was looking around in that vigilant way she remembered. He was always on alert, always ready for danger.

Thank God for men like him.

Against her better judgment, she leaned her face into his chest as they walked and inhaled his spicy masculine scent. She didn't care if she looked crazy; she wanted to roll around in that purely male essence. Vincent just brought out that primal, extremely feminine part of her and after living like a nun for so long, she wanted to find pleasure with him. Hours and hours of it. More like days and weeks and... nope, not going down that path. She couldn't expect more than a few nights with him. Deep down she was pretty sure he'd never get over the way she'd left and while it killed her, she still wanted to take what he could offer. She wanted something to hold onto as she tried to figure her life out again.

His arm tightened around her as they turned at the next corner. "You're killing me, Jordan," he murmured, still not looking at her.

She wasn't sure of his tone, and since he was still scanning their surroundings, she couldn't read his expression. "How?"

He snorted softly before turning to face her and slowly backing her up against a high stone wall that hid a house. The way he moved reminded her of a skilled predator, as if he was stalking his prey. Of course she didn't mind being his prey. Not when she had firsthand experience with the kind of pleasure he could deliver. Her bare upper back slightly scraped against the rough stone, but she hardly noticed.

The street was much quieter than where they'd just come from, with cars and mopeds parked along the curb. Out of the corner of her eye she spotted a couple across the street walking in the other direction, with their backs to her and Vincent. But no one else.

As he watched her with a hot, assessing stare and pale blue eyes that still captivated her, she could hear upbeat reggae style music in the distance, but all her focus was on the man in front of her—the way his chest rose and fell in an unsteady rhythm, the body heat he emanated, his spicy scent. She just wanted to lean into him and soak him up. He placed his hands on the wall on either side of her, caging her in, and rolled his hips once against her.

Oh my. His erection pressed insistently against her, letting her know how much he wanted her, but with the exception of his clear lust, his expression was hard to read. Maybe this was just about sex for him. His breathing was slightly erratic as he watched her. Her gaze drifted to his lips. Why was he just standing there? Unable to read his exact mood and afraid of his rejection, she didn't have the courage to lift up on her tiptoes and kiss him. Though she really wanted to.

"What are you thinking?" he murmured as a cool

breeze ruffled around them. It might be July, but being surrounded by water on all sides, there was a constant flow of air.

"I'm wondering if you're going to kiss me or not."

"I know what I did at the condo earlier and I swear I'm not trying to give you mixed signals. I just don't want to take things too fast between us. Not until..." Sighing, he trailed off and looked away from her for a moment.

The line of his jaw was hard, clenched. She wanted to reach up and trace it with her finger, but resisted the urge. She had a feeling she understood what he wasn't saying out loud. He didn't want to cross a line until he knew what he wanted between them. Which she actually understood. But it didn't mean that it hurt less. She couldn't change the past, couldn't change her decision. Knowing what she did now, she wasn't so sure she'd have made the same decision. Probably not, considering how much she ached at the moment. She'd tried for so damn long to get over him and she never truly had. She'd just compartmentalized. Unfortunately that wasn't working anymore.

When he'd ordered her out of his home in Miami it had been cutting, but she'd been prepared to deal with it. Now that he'd followed her, her emotions were a mess. "Let's just get out of here," she muttered, not wanting to stand there a second longer, her body and heart craving what they couldn't have.

"Hold on." His voice was low and harsh and his body had gone suddenly rigid.

Peering around him, she spotted a driver covered from head to toe in all black gear riding a moped. It was strange considering it was July, but the person had on a long-sleeved T-shirt, a helmet with dark tint and...what the hell?

Jordan blinked, not sure what she was seeing. It

almost looked as if flames were coming up on the other side of the bike. Was it on fire? Wanting to help, she shoved away from the wall, but Vincent held her in place.

She started to ask him what he was doing when she realized the bike wasn't on fire. The driver was holding a bottle and it had flames rolling off the top. It was a freaking Molotov cocktail. The driver hauled back an arm, poised like a pitcher, ready to throw it right at them!

Her body tensed, her heart rate going into overdrive, but before she could react, Vincent cursed and tackled her to the ground. All the air whooshed out of her lungs as an explosion of fire and glass crashed against the wall above them. Shards rained down on them as Vincent rolled them away, taking the brunt of the falling pieces just as a second explosion of fire shattered lower against the wall.

The sidewalk was unforgiving against their bodies as Vincent kept rolling them until they ran into a parked car. Though adrenaline was raging through her system, she wasn't hurt except for a few scrapes on her elbows.

Vincent pushed off her before she could take stock of him. He jumped to his feet, every line of his body pulled taut as if he was ready to take off after the attacker on foot. But the squeal of tires had him cursing. Heart thundering, she started to follow his lead, then he crouched down to where she sat on the edge of the sidewalk.

He gently cupped her cheek as he assessed her face then scanned her body. "Baby, are you hurt anywhere?"

She swallowed, struggled to find her voice. "No, just…stunned. Did someone actually throw a Molotov cocktail at us? That's insane."

His jaw was tight as he nodded. "They took off but I got the license plate." He glanced around again at the sound of footsteps pounding the pavement behind them.

"Are you guys all right?" Two college aged boys with dark tans wearing only board shorts and flip-flops hurried down the sidewalk toward them.

"We're good, thanks." Vincent said as he helped her to her feet.

An uncontrollable shake rippled through her.

"We called the cops," one of them said. His blond hair was spiked and messy.

"Thanks," Vincent murmured.

Jeez, the cops. Of course. She wasn't even thinking straight. Wasn't thinking at all. She looked up at Vincent. "Did you get hurt?" She realized she hadn't even asked him that.

His expression was soft as he shook his head. "No, baby. I've been in worse scrapes than this."

She knew he had. Still, she stepped back and ran her hands down his arms then over his chest, inspecting him, needing him to be okay. What if one of those bottles had hit him? Or both of them? God, they would have been—

"Stop." That one word was a harsh order.

"What?" Even her voice trembled. She inwardly cursed herself. He was being so stoic and she felt like a shaking mess of nerves.

"I can see you're playing the 'what if' game in your head. Don't do it. We're fine and unharmed. No one's ever going to fucking hurt you." He spoke with such authority that some of the fear pulsing through her dissipated.

But not completely. What the hell was wrong with people? After living seven years in fear for her life, this random act of violence stunned her so deeply.

She was vaguely aware of the two surfer looking guys talking a couple yards down in hushed tones, but she kept her focus on Vincent and nodded. "Okay, we're safe. That's what matters."

Instead of responding, he pulled her into a tight embrace and she wasn't sure if it was her imagination, but it almost felt like he trembled when he hugged her.

* * * * *

That had gone perfectly. Gauging the reaction time of Jordan's friend had been a plus, but terrifying that bitch had been even better. This was going to be so much fun.

And so worth it when Jordan finally got what was coming to her. Unfortunately the man with her had reacted quickly and expertly, moving with an impressive speed as he'd quickly gotten both of them to cover. He'd also been very protective of Jordan. After this attack, her friend—or more likely lover—would probably be vigilant in keeping her protected.

Even if they assumed it was a random attack, their guards would be up, especially the man's. It wouldn't matter in the end because Jordan would die.

The manner of her death was still undecided, however. Killing her with a simple bullet would be too easy for Jordan. No, she needed to suffer. Hopefully by fire. Curtis's favorite method. But drowning could work too.

Figuring out who Jordan's friend was first, had become a priority though. Well, a priority after ditching the stolen moped. Key West had enough CCTV's that losing the bike and changing clothes was a necessity.

Then tomorrow the next steps in terrifying Jordan would begin. There was no guarantee she'd be staying in Key West for long. She might go back to Miami with the unknown male, making another attack more difficult. No, that bitch was going to die right in Key West.

Chapter 5

"I'll be right back," Vincent murmured before dropping a quick kiss on Jordan's forehead.

She just nodded, stress lines bracketing her mouth. He didn't like leaving her, even for a second, but she was sitting safely in a detective's office and he could see her through the open blinds of the window while he stepped out into the bullpen of the Key West police department. It wasn't as loud as he'd expected, though there was a quiet buzz of constant movement as people did their jobs. This was the last place he wanted to be, but there was no way around it. They'd had to make an official statement, which meant paperwork. Luckily the chief knew of Red Stone Security and had worked with a bunch of different government agencies before so he was cooperative.

That attitude had clearly been adopted by his subordinates as well. Or at least the men and women Vincent had come in contact with tonight, including Detective Leon Hough.

Hough was talking to a uniformed officer next to a community coffee station, but nodded and broke away when he saw Vincent step out. "You or Ms. Alvarado want any coffee or water?" he asked as soon as he reached him.

"No, we're good, but thanks. She just wants to get out of here. I appreciate you talking to me privately." He'd asked for a moment of the man's time before they left in the hopes that he could garner some insight into why they'd been attacked. If this type of thing had happened before in the area it would actually make him feel better. But if it had been a targeted attack…that brought up new concerns.

The dark haired man nodded. "I understand. So what's up?"

"I know you can't talk about ongoing investigations and I'm not asking because I want to take the law into my own hands, but have there been any similar incidents lately? Any racially motivated crimes?" Though he'd dealt with his share of racism, he'd found those types of crimes to be rare. Still, he wanted to cover all bases.

The detective snorted and shook his head. "Not down here. At least not with the locals. We all have a live and let live attitude, but with tourists you never know. But no, we haven't had any reports of someone using firebombs as a weapon. That kind of attack is strange."

"Yeah, I know." He'd doubted the race angle, but had wanted to check. In his broad experience, people generally killed for similar reasons; love, revenge and money. People were simple like that. Obviously there were other reasons, especially with hate motivated crimes and religious nuts, but in the civilian world things tended to be simpler. And what had happened tonight had felt almost personal. That kind of attack just wasn't normal.

"Wish I had more for you." The detective sounded sincere.

Sighing, he scrubbed a hand over his face. "Me, too.

Thanks though .You've got our contact info and where we're both staying. Call me day or night if anything pops up." He hoped what had happened was just a random act of violence and they could move past it, but he still planned to be careful.

Something had shifted in him tonight and it was all because of Jordan. He still felt so damn shaky he was surprised no one else noticed. His heart rate was higher than normal and his fucking palms were actually sweating. Vincent always kept his cool, but the thought of anything happening to Jordan—especially on his watch—made him fucking crazy.

While he hated what had happened, it had made his decision about her easy. He wasn't walking away. He couldn't live knowing she was off somewhere and not be with her. Nope. Not gonna happen.

The sexy woman belonged to him. Very soon he was going to remind her why.

He popped his head back in the room and she immediately stood, wrapping her arms around herself like she did when she was nervous or scared. It pierced him to see her like that and he wanted to hurt the person who had caused it. "Can we go?"

"Yeah." He held out his arm and she walked right into his embrace, wrapping her arm around his waist as he led her out.

The feel of her pressed up against him and the fact that she didn't hesitate in searching him out for comfort had the ability to bring him to his knees.

"Did the detective say anything else? Do they have any leads?" There was a thread of hope in her voice.

Hating to disappoint her, he shook his head as they stepped out into the balmy night air. "Unfortunately, no." He had plans to look more into the monster who had changed her life, Curtis Woods. Vincent didn't care that the FBI said Woods and his brother were dead; he wanted to make damn sure that was true. Not to mention he had some potential enemies and he was worried this might be one of them trying to mess with him. "I need to stop by my place and grab an overnight bag and my laptop, but it's not a long walk."

She looked up at him in surprise. "You're staying with me tonight?"

He grunted. How could she not realize he was staying with her? "Of course. After what happened, I'm not letting you out of my sight."

Something he couldn't read flickered through her hazel eyes as she looked away, keeping her gaze focused in front of them on the sidewalk. "I don't need you feeling responsible for me. That attack was crazy, but I can take care of myself. I've been doing it for a long time."

Responsible? She really had no idea. "Yeah, well, that's about to change." He wanted to take care of her any way he could.

She stopped in the middle of the sidewalk and pulled away from him. "Vincent, I can't do this. I…thought I could, but I can't. All I really wanted was your forgiveness when I came to see you—okay, that's a lie, I wanted more—but that's not the point. I just can't sleep with you and have it mean nothing. I thought I could, but I can't. And if you stay the night I know where things are headed between us." There was such raw agony in her voice, it cut him impossibly deep.

Vincent swallowed hard, trying to make his throat work. He didn't want just sex either, but he also knew that telling her that wouldn't do him much good. Not when only hours ago he'd admitted he was trying to figure things out where they were concerned. Now he knew exactly what he wanted from her. Everything. When that asshole had thrown that firebomb at them, he'd lost a decade of his life and the reality of what he needed—Jordan, in his life, forever—had become crystal clear. He wouldn't lose her again. But words were useless.

He would have to show her, not tell her. "I'll sleep on the couch, but I'm not letting you out of my sight."

For a moment it looked as if she might argue, but she finally nodded. "Fine." Instead of wrapping her arm back around him, she kept her arms tightly around herself as they headed to his place.

* * * * *

Jordan felt as if her emotions were on a freaking tilt-a-whirl. Completely out of control and making her just a little bit nauseous. She pulled her knees up to her chest and wrapped her arms around them as she sat on the couch and half listened to Vincent's conversation. He was talking to someone he worked with. A woman. Jordan could tell because of the softer tone of his voice. Even if she hadn't heard Vincent originally talking to the woman's husband, she would have known.

He was always like that. Back when they'd been dating she could always tell if he was talking to his mom or one of his sisters. Whenever that happened, he seemed almost docile, like a little puppy. Jordan had always wondered what kind of woman it would take to make a man like Vincent be on his best behavior. Sadly she'd never gotten the chance to meet his family. And right about now, Jordan had a feeling she never would.

Not with the way things were headed between her and Vincent. She sure as hell didn't want to be his responsibility and that's what he was treating her like. They'd been randomly attacked but she wasn't worried about some maniac breaking into her place. Hardly anyone knew she was here. The man she'd put behind bars and his brother that she'd feared for so long were both dead. There was no one left to hurt her.

After what felt like an eternity, Vincent finally ended his phone call. Leaning forward on the couch, he set his phone on the coffee table between them and rubbed a hand over his hair. It was still just as short as it had been seven years ago. His habit of rubbing his head when he was agitated hadn't changed either.

"So what did your friend say?" She couldn't stand the suspense.

He looked up at her and pinned her with that pale stare. "Lizzy is going to look into all my old files, see if anything sticks out. I had a few brushes with assholes on various cases, but nothing to warrant the kind of attack we had tonight. And nothing recent. That type of raw violence just doesn't make sense." She could see the wheels turning in his head as he looked at her and she realized he wasn't really seeing her, but thinking.

"Sometimes crazy just doesn't make sense." She'd lived for years in a semi-state of fear. It didn't matter that she'd been in WITSEC, that fear had taken root deep inside her and she refused to live like that again. Hell no. She was finally free and was determined to actually live that way.

"Yeah, maybe," he muttered before opening his laptop.

Frowning, she glanced at the nautical themed clock that was made to look like a porthole on the wall next to the sliding glass door. "It's almost midnight, why don't you get some rest?" There were two bedrooms, both with queen sized beds, so he'd have plenty of room to stretch out.

He grunted a non-response and fired up his laptop anyway. Sighing, she stood. She knew better than to argue with him when he was determined about something. The man could be damn stubborn when he wanted. She headed to the kitchen and made a half pot of coffee. If he was going to be up, she figured she could at least do something. Once it was brewed, she poured him a mug, but found the living room empty.

Jordan set the mug on the side table and glanced at his computer screen. A file had been pulled up that almost looked like a mug shot of a woman. A very beautiful blonde woman. Next to the picture was a bunch of text. She started to scan it when she heard a door shut.

Vincent appeared from the hallway moments later. His eyes lit up when he saw the mug. "You made coffee?"

"Yep, just the way you like it." Two scoops of sugar, nothing more.

He grinned in such a boyish way, she forgot about pretty much everything for a few seconds. She really hated the effect he had on her. It was as if she forgot to breathe sometimes. "Who's the woman? Is she important?" Jordan asked, motioning to the open laptop.

That sexy smile suddenly fell as he shook his head. "No."

At that, she raised her eyebrows. "No, what? She's not important? Obviously she is or you wouldn't be wasting time on whatever that file is. Come on, don't leave me in the dark if you know something about tonight." It wasn't like she needed to be protected from whatever he thought was going on. After what she'd been through, she could handle pretty much anything.

"She's...just some woman I dated a while ago. She went kind of stalker on me and I had to take out a restraining order. I haven't seen her in almost two years and haven't had any issues, but I had Lizzy run her records to see where she's been hanging out lately." He said the words in a rush, glancing back at the screen as he spoke.

Jordan knew that Vincent had dated. Probably a whole lot. It made sense and she had no reason to get mad. She was the one who'd left. She'd made that choice. But it still hurt to actually hear that he'd been with other women. And she knew it was beyond stupid to feel hurt, but she did just the same. For years she'd locked down thoughts of Vincent completely, had locked down stupid masochistic images of him with other women. Actually seeing someone he'd been with felt like a punch to the stomach. Not to mention the woman looked so damn different from her. Jordan wasn't sure why that was worse, but somehow it was. "Covering all bases is good." Damn it, why did her voice have to tremble? Swallowing hard, she tilted her head in the direction of the bedrooms. "If you don't need me, I'm going to crash."

Without waiting for a response, she made a quick escape. Tonight had left her feeling raw and vulnerable and she simply couldn't add any more to her plate. Sleep was the only thing that might make her feel better. Unfortunately she had a feeling finding rest was going to be difficult.

Chapter 6

Jordan stared at the ceiling in the darkened bedroom. She'd pulled the drapes back from the sliding glass door so that the room was illuminated by moonlight and a few stars. Both bedrooms had private balconies looking out over the pool at the complex. She wondered if Vincent had his curtains open too.

Okay, she didn't care about the state of his stupid windows. She wanted to know if he was sleeping naked or not. About an hour ago she'd finally heard him go to his room. She wasn't sure what he'd been doing on his laptop but he'd eventually given up. For that she was thankful. He'd looked so exhausted earlier.

She was annoyed with herself because her body was begging for rest but her mind was working overtime, refusing to let her give in to the call of sleep. Shoving off the sheets, she slid out of bed. The cool hardwood floor chilled her feet as she made her way across the nautical themed room. Maybe a hot cup of herbal tea would help, though she doubted it. But at three in the morning, she was willing to try anything.

The place seemed so silent as she strode down the

hallway. As she started to pass Vincent's room a muffled, almost strangled sound made her pause. Then she heard it again and it was definitely coming from his room.

A wave of anxiety swelled through her. After what had happened only hours ago, she was feeling edgy. The door had been left cracked open a few inches so she nudged it and stepped inside.

This room had more of a beach theme than nautical. A salvaged piece of driftwood had been treated and was displayed above the bed, holding a collection of sea coral. And Vincent was curled up on his side in the middle of the queen sized bed under the display. With his back to her, he looked tense, all his muscles pulled tight. The moonlight spilled in from the glass doors, illuminating his toned, powerful body.

When he let out another strangled moan she hurried to his side. Kneeling on the edge of the bed, she gently touched his shoulder in the hopes of pulling him out of whatever was going on inside his head. She hated the thought of him being in any kind of anguish, even while asleep. His skin was warm under her fingertips.

At her touch, he stilled and she let out a small sigh of relief. She started to get off the bed, but nearly had a heart attack when Vincent shot up in bed. Yelping, she tried to move back, but he was fast and in seconds had her pinned underneath him.

Breathing hard, with his hands on her shoulders in a tight grip, he stared at her with those pale eyes. But he wasn't really seeing her. It was almost as if he was looking through her.

"Vincent, are you awake?" she whispered.

At her voice, he seemed to shake out of whatever was going on. Blinking, he shook his head as if clearing away the vision of something. He stared down at her in confusion. "Jordan, what are you…?" He looked at his hands, then down at their bodies where he was splayed over her, and back up to her face.

"I think you were having a bad dream or something. I was just checking on you." She kept her voice low.

"Did I hurt you?" he asked as he loosened his fingers from her shoulders, but didn't take them off completely. Instead, he gently caressed his hands down her bare arms.

"No, I was worried. Do you want to talk about it?" Knowing him, she doubted it.

Shaking his head, he pushed up and rolled off her. Immediately she missed the feel of his muscular body covering hers, but she didn't have time to dwell on it. As he lay back against the pillows, he practically dragged her over him so that she was half-laying on his chest.

She knew she should probably leave the room and definitely not get all physically tangled up with him, but her body wouldn't listen. Nope, she liked being gathered in Vincent's arms. She laid her cheek against his chest and when he linked his fingers through hers and placed their hands over his stomach, she knew she wasn't going anywhere tonight. His breathing was slightly erratic and she could hear the jagged beat of his heart as he came down from whatever internal adrenaline rush he'd had.

"Sorry if I woke you up. It...I think the fire bomb from earlier must have triggered a memory. I was having a dream about an op that didn't turn out so well." His voice was ragged as he spoke and she could hear the pain in his voice. Vincent had never talked much about his time in the Navy and she'd always respected his privacy.

But she still wanted to be there for him. "You can tell me about it if you want."

"I know, I just can't. Classified stuff." Now there was sadness laced through his words.

Which made her heart ache knowing how much he

had to keep bottled up inside. Since he wouldn't be able to tell her anything about past operations, she didn't push. Instead she said, "Tell me a good memory. Funny or happy."

He was silent for a long moment, his breathing slowly evening out. She wondered if he'd speak, but eventually he did. "Right around the time I turned thirteen, I had a growth spurt and thought I was pretty hot shit." He chuckled lightly, the sound wrapping around her like a warm embrace. She loved to hear him laugh. "I was playing ball with some of the older guys in my neighborhood one evening and my mom came out to tell me it was dinner time. I can't remember exactly what I said, but I mouthed off to her. This was before my dad died, but he was out of town, and I knew she was dealing with my sisters' boy drama—they were all teenagers at the same time—and I thought I could get away with being a little punk. She didn't say anything that night but the next morning when she took me to school she didn't change out of her pajamas and she had on some hideous slippers with pink horses on them. I think she snagged them from one of my sisters—who, incidentally, had all gotten rides to school with their friends that morning. Traitors," he muttered.

"But she wasn't done. Oh no, not my mama. She put on a housecoat I'm pretty sure belonged to my grandmother, a shower cap, and told me to get in the van. When I asked her what she was doing she said that if I was going to act as if she embarrassed me, she'd give me a reason to be embarrassed. She also said that if I couldn't respect my own mother in front of my friends that she clearly wasn't raising me right and was going to make some changes."

Jordan laughed against his chest, unable to contain her howl of amusement. When she looked into Vincent's face, his lips were quirked up at the corners. "So what happened?" she asked.

He shook his head, but he was smiling. "She took me to school, and stubborn little ass that I was, I didn't think she'd actually go through with getting out of the car, but that woman has no fear. As she started to get out I apologized—profusely—and begged forgiveness. She told me if I ever mouthed off to her in front of anyone again, I couldn't even imagine what she'd do. That's the day I realized that my mother is smarter and scarier than I'll ever be."

Jordan grinned up at him. "She sounds like a trip."

"That, she is. My sister Zoe still hasn't learned her lesson where my mom is concerned, but that's probably because she's just as scary as my mom."

"I'd love to meet them." The words slipped out before she could rein in her big mouth. She inwardly cringed and tried to think of a way to backpedal what she'd said.

"I'd like that too." Now there was no amusement on his face. Just a raw intensity that stole her breath.

She had no idea what to make of that comment. Absolutely. No. Clue.

"Over the past few years, there have been other women in my life." His abrupt change in topic was like a knife in her chest.

She so did not need to hear any of this. Even if it was true, she didn't want to hear the fucking words. Jordan started to get up, but he held her firm, his grip around her tightening. "Why the hell are you telling me this?" she snarled, not bothering to hide her hurt.

"Because I don't want anything between us. There might have been others in my life, but no one *meant* anything to me. I never got over you. When you left, it was like you took part of me with you."

Tears burned her eyes. She didn't want to hear this either. Didn't want him to tell her how much she'd hurt him, even if she had. She could feel her emotions spiraling out of control and didn't want to break down in front of him. Blinking the wetness away, she kept her gaze on his. In the moonlight, his beautiful pale eyes seemed even brighter against his dark skin. "You can't know how sorry I am," she whispered.

"I'm not telling you because I want an apology. I wasn't sure if I'd be able to get over you leaving, but after last night, I'm not living without you, Jordan. I…can't. And I don't want to."

She could hear the truth in his voice, but she also knew he could be saying this now and mean it, but what happened later? What happened when he couldn't get over what she'd done? Just a few hours ago he hadn't been sure what the hell he wanted and now he was so positive? *No freaking way.* She tried to tell herself to get the hell out of his room, to get far away from him before they crossed a line and she got her heart shattered. Walking away had nearly killed her.

If he walked out on her after this, she didn't know that she'd survive the heartbreak.

Before she could form a response or force herself to leave the room, he kissed her. Maybe he'd sensed her hesitation, she wasn't sure, but he moved lightning fast, crushing his lips over hers in a heated, hungry kiss— devouring her mouth. It was the only way she could describe what he was doing to her. Like he was trying to completely possess her.

He shifted in an impressively quick move so that his body was on top of hers, pinning her to the bed once again. This time he was fully awake and aware of what he was doing. And she loved the feel of him on her more than anything. As his mouth and tongue teased hers, he slid one of his hands through her hair until he was cupping her head in a dominating grip that was so familiar it made her chest ache.

She wasn't about to stop what was happening between them. Even if it would be better for her in the end, she needed to be with him again, needed to experience everything Vincent had to offer. When he rolled his hips against hers, his hard length pressing against the juncture between her thighs, she moaned into his mouth. She hated that her pajama pants and his boxers were in the way when all she wanted was to feel him sliding deep inside her.

It had been too damn long since she'd taken real pleasure and she wanted it so badly. But only from him. Only from Vincent.

Her hands skated over his taut shoulders then down his bare chest. The feel of all that raw power under her fingertips made her entire body shudder and tighten in awareness. It was hard not to be aware of this man. Of everything he made her feel and want.

"Fuck yeah, touch me everywhere, baby," he whispered as he tore his mouth from hers. He feathered kisses along her jaw in a slow, sensuous path that made her inner walls tighten with unfulfilled need.

Following his directive, she slid one of her hands under the waistband of his boxers and fisted his cock. No teasing right now. He pulsed in her hand as she stroked him once. The way he groaned against her ear and shuddered gave her a feeling of such power that she'd only ever experienced with him.

She loved bringing this man to his knees. Because he could do the same to her so easily. Literally and figuratively.

Even though she wanted to continue stroking his erection, she wanted him out of his clothes first. She wanted to see exactly what she'd been fantasizing about for so long. Removing her hand, she bunched the material of his boxers at the sides and started shoving them down his hips as he continued kissing her neck and chest. Thankfully he helped getting them the rest of the way off and kicked them away.

The feel of his lips along her skin was pushing her into sensory overload and suddenly she couldn't stand it anymore. Reaching for the hem of her tank top, she grabbed it and practically tore it off. For a brief moment, she felt completely exposed. Which seemed stupid since he'd seen her naked not too long ago. But still, it had been years and now they weren't rushing into this like maniacs. She had time to think about what they were doing and she was very conscious of her body and the fact that she wasn't twenty-two anymore.

Vincent had made a protesting sound until he realized what she was doing. Now he knelt in between her spread legs, his cock pulsing upward in such a beautiful display that she had to bite back her moan of need. She couldn't wait to feel that thickness pushing inside her. Had dreamt about it for way too long.

Her bottoms were still on, but with her breasts bared to him, he looked almost ravenous. The glint in his gaze sent another wave of hunger rolling through her. Squirming under his intensity, her nipples tightened to almost painful points as he let out a low curse.

"God, baby, I've been fantasizing about this for so long. Too fucking long," he murmured before bending his head to capture one of her breasts with his mouth. His tongue teased and licked along the underside of her sensitive skin before he found her nipple and sucked. Hard.

The sharp action made her back arch off the bed and she wrapped her legs around him. *Stupid pants were still in the way.*

She wanted to take them off, but wanted to touch him more. Needed it. Craved it. She spread her fingers over his head, savoring the feel of holding him as he flicked his tongue over the tight bud of her nipple. His hair was buzzed almost to his skull so she grabbed onto his head, holding him in place.

He just chuckled against her sensitive nipple and slightly pulled his head back. "I'm not going anywhere."

Was that a promise in those gorgeous eyes? She swallowed hard, unable to find her voice before he dipped his head again to her other breast. He lavished that one with just as much attention. With each stroke of his tongue, she felt the pulse between her legs grow hotter and more insistent.

Somehow she forced her hands from his head and slowly stroked her fingers down his back. His taut muscles tensed under her touch, his big body trembling.

When he started a path down her belly she knew what he intended. And while she wanted to feel his mouth on her again, she wanted to feel him inside her even more. They could drag out the foreplay for hours later. Right now, she was walking a tightrope of control and she was about to lose it. "No," she rasped out as he grasped the edge of her pajama bottoms with his hands.

Hovering over her, he looked up, his eyes wide in confusion. "You don't want this?" His voice was ragged.

"No, yes, I do, I just mean no foreplay. I want you in me. Now." Her face flamed as he watched her with a mix of hunger and amusement. She was practically rabid to have him in her and he seemed almost unaffected. Of course his hard cock said otherwise, but still, it was maddening how in control he appeared.

"I forgot how impatient you are," he murmured as he tugged her bottoms and panties down her legs. When his gaze landed on her mound, she squirmed under his intensity. "Should I tease you?" he asked, his eyes pinned to hers as he dragged a finger along the length of her wet slit.

He didn't penetrate though, just stroked up and down in languorous movements. Damn him. He *was* going to tease her.

"Payback will suck," she promised. Because she could tease him until he was begging. The thought of doing so made her even wetter.

Finally, he pushed two fingers inside her in one long stroke. His eyes shut for a moment as he pulled out then pushed back in.

She slightly arched her back off the bed as her inner walls clenched around him and she let her own eyes close. It wasn't enough, she needed so much more. When he completely withdrew, her eyes snapped open to find him watching her intently.

He put his fingers in his mouth, the act of him tasting her incredibly erotic. "I don't think I will tease you." His voice shook as he spoke and she realized he was just as close to losing it as she was. *Thank God.*

She couldn't take any more torture.

When he slid off the bed she worried he was stopping, but then realized he was grabbing a condom from his bag.

"I'm on the Pill," she blurted. She'd been on it forever because it kept her regulated. If not, she had too many not-fun issues. Since she hadn't been with anyone since him, she was obviously clean and didn't need to spell it out.

Vincent dropped his bag as if it was on fire and turned to face her. With the moonlight bathing him, he looked like an ancient warrior standing there; his thighs, stomach and chest all toned muscles and so much perfection she could barely stand it. He might as well have been cut from marble. He cleared his throat once and stepped back toward the bed like a panther stalking his prey. "I'm tested every six months and haven't been with anyone since my last two tests. And I've never gone without a condom. Except…"

With her. She knew that was what he couldn't seem

to say. She reached out her arms to him and he practically pounced on her, his tongue tangling with hers as he cupped her head in the way she loved. She could taste herself on him and found it wildly erotic.

His strong chest rubbed against her breasts as they kissed, the friction stimulating her nipples and working her up even more. She wrapped her legs tight around his waist, grinding against him and soaking up his heat.

He'd already tested her slickness so she wasn't surprised when he thrust inside her without further teasing. She was, however, surprised by how full she felt. All the air rushed from her lungs in one whoosh as he stilled and she adjusted to his size. Pulling his head back, he looked down at her, faint concern etched on his handsome face.

"You okay?" he whispered.

Unable to find her voice, she nodded. She was more than okay. She felt absolutely amazing. Her inner walls clenched and tightened around him, molding to his thick length as she pumped her hips against his once.

That was all the incentive he needed to start moving. She clutched onto his back as he began thrusting in an intense rhythm she could barely keep up with. When he reached between their bodies and tweaked her clit with his thumb and forefinger, she surged into orgasm.

The sharp climax took her off guard. For so long she'd used her hand to get off and she had the movements down to an art. But this was nothing like her self-pleasuring.

As Vincent slammed into her over and over, her orgasm pitched higher and higher as pure bliss hit all her nerve endings. Closing her eyes, she moaned and let her head fall back against the pillow as it continued to punch through her, battering her senses with no reprieve.

Letting out his own shout, he buried his face against her neck and groaned as he released himself inside her.

His warmth filled her and she dug her fingers into his backside as his thrusts slowed, only letting up when he finally stilled inside her.

Breathing hard, she could feel the erratic beat of his heart. Her body protested when he lifted off her, but she realized he wasn't going far. He propped up on his forearms to look down at her, his expression one of a supremely satisfied male. "Next time I'm teasing you until you beg."

Grinning, she lightly pinched his behind. She was just glad there was going to be a next time. She still had no clue what was going to happen between them or what kind of future they could even have, but she was going to soak up every second of this time with Vincent that she could.

But the truth was, no matter what, she wasn't giving him up without a fight. As he'd climaxed inside her, the knowledge had slammed into her as hard as her own orgasm. She'd sacrificed him once, she wasn't doing it again.

Chapter 7

The parking lot of Jordan's condo complex was quiet in the pre-dawn hours. Patience was a virtue and after hours of waiting for the right moment, it had arrived. No drunken revelers or late night stragglers to see something they shouldn't. Eliminating others wasn't a problem, but right now Jordan was the focus.

Her pain and torment were all that mattered.

Getting under Jordan's car was easy enough. Planting the plastic explosives was a different story. Curtis had always been in charge of bombs and rigging any fires to start. But, it was beyond time to step up and get more hands-on experience.

At least C4 was easy to handle and stable. You could drop it, jump up and down on it or even shoot it and it wouldn't detonate. Nope, it needed an excessive amount of heat and a detonator.

This is where things got tricky; inserting the blasting caps. Coming by these had been slightly easier than originally planned. After breaking into an excavation site, locating and stealing the blasting caps had been simple. Killing that guard had been necessary and enjoyable. It was always a thrill to watch the life drain from someone's eyes. To feel that power of holding someone's life in your hands.

After connecting the wires to a cheap throw away cell phone, sliding the thin cylindrical detonators into place was a sensitive job. *God, why won't my hands stop shaking?*

Once the two caps were in and the coast was clear, getting a safe distance away was paramount. That was what Curtis had always said. Bombs and fire were beautiful, but to be respected. Curtis had talked about boosters in detonators before and how they could make a blasting cap more sensitive and powerful, but there was no way to tell if these had them.

Oh well, soon enough either this would work or it wouldn't. And Jordan's lover would be a burning carcass.

* * * * *

As warmth spread over her face, Jordan opened her eyes to the sun bathing the bed in a blanket of heat. Rolling over, she frowned to find Vincent's side empty. But when the delicious aroma of coffee hit her, she smiled.

She didn't function well without caffeine, something he knew. Stretching her arms over her head, she savored the delicious soreness spreading through her body. After their first time last night, Vincent hadn't been even close to done. The man had been almost savage in how much he'd wanted her.

He'd taken everything she had and she'd given it freely. Being with him again had been a stark reminder to her body what she'd been missing all these years. The idea of giving it up, of giving him up—no way.

After taking a long, hot shower and brushing her

teeth, she changed into one of her bikinis and threw on a light summer dress that tied around her neck. She had no idea what their plans were for the day but she hoped it included sun, sand and a whole lot of sex.

She'd forgo the first two for the sex though, hands down.

When she found Vincent in the kitchen cooking— shirtless—her breath caught in her throat. With his back to her and all the natural light flooding the room, his body was illuminated like the warrior god he might as well be. All those taut, perfect lines made her mouth water. As her gaze tracked his body, she was instantly drawn to his scars. They were faint, but she knew what they were. Some were from knife wounds. Another webbed section of skin at the top of his shoulder she was pretty certain was a bullet wound. But he'd never confirmed it when she'd asked him. He'd just said that he couldn't talk about it. That by itself had been a confirmation of sorts.

That *body*. Pre-coffee, it was too much to even focus on. "You better put a shirt on unless you want to get jumped," she murmured as she stepped into the room. The cool tile felt good against her bare feet.

He half-turned from where he stood at the stove cooking something that smelled delicious and his lazy, predatory grin stole the rest of her breath. "Jump away."

She watched him for a long moment, her heart beating wildly and the dampness between her thighs already growing because of a single, heated look. Shaking her head, she smiled at him. "I will—after you feed me and I get coffee. You tired me out last night." She felt a blush creeping across her cheeks at the admission. It was the best kind of exhaustion, but still, she needed sustenance.

Of course his grin just grew in that totally smug male way as he turned back to the stove. "We're not even close to done, baby."

She certainly hoped not. "So…what's on the agenda for today? Are you able to stay in Key West for a little while?" she asked as she snagged a coffee mug, hoping her question sounded casual when it was anything but. They hadn't talked much last night and she wasn't sure what was going to happen between them now.

"I've built up a lot of vacation days and I've already let my boss know I'll be taking time off for a while."

A while, what did that mean? She wanted to push but felt weird doing so. Years ago she'd been comfortable asking him anything, but right now things were still unsettled between them. At least that's how she felt. But she could focus on the positive. He was staying in town, which meant they got to spend more time together. "Want to be geeky tourists today? Head down to one of the beaches, then hit up the shops on Duval?" He'd probably hate the shopping part, but she threw it in there anyway.

"How about instead of shopping, we go parasailing or jet skiing?" he asked as he pulled the pan off the stove. When he moved she saw a plate of bacon he'd already cooked. It was that delicious scent that had her stomach rumbling.

Jordan sat at one of the high top chairs at the counter with her coffee. "Sounds fun, but let's do both. Parasailing, then jet skiing." She was ready to have fun and stop feeling like she had to look over her shoulder all the time.

"Works for me, but first you're eating. Then…" he trailed off as he pulled two plates down from one of the cabinets.

She knew exactly what would happen after they ate and she wasn't complaining. "You're part machine, I swear."

He snorted as he started piling bacon and scrambled

eggs onto their plates. "Now that I've got you under the same roof, I'm taking advantage."

Her toes curled at the almost ragged way he said that. Before she could respond, he continued. "Want any toast?"

She shook her head as she watched him move around the kitchen. A man cooking was just plain sexy all by itself, but Vincent cooking—shirtless—yeah, she was going to have a freaking heart attack. All her coffee had done was wake her up and now she was even more aware of the deliciousness that was Vincent.

As he slid a plate piled with way too much food in front of her, he took his own seat and gave her a look she couldn't quite define. It was almost assessing. "This looks amazing, thanks for cooking—and for making coffee."

He half-smiled and her heart rate jumped up a notch. "I remember what a monster you are without caffeine."

It was true, so she ignored the statement as she took a bite of bacon. Sweet heaven. Awesome sex and great food. She could get used to this, even if she was afraid to.

"How long do you plan to stay down here? And what do you plan to do now that you're not in hiding anymore?" Vincent's softly asked questions were like bombs going off in the quiet room.

Jordan turned to look at him again and found that same assessing expression on his face. She had no clue what she was going to do—but she did know she wanted to spend as much time with him as possible. "I don't know. This summer I'm hoping to figure out where I want to live and work and all that fun stuff. I've got some money saved and I'm basically staying here for free so…" She shrugged.

"You plan to teach again?" He hadn't even touched his food.

The way he was watching her was almost unnerving. She hated that he'd gone from sensual, teasing Vincent to being unreadable. He didn't look angry or anything, but it still jarred her. "Yes. I love it." And there wasn't anything else she'd ever had a drive to do. When she'd been in college getting her degree, she'd thought she wanted to teach younger kids but after her time in New Mexico she realized high school was the right age range for her.

"There are plenty of teaching jobs in Miami," he said casually before turning all his attention to his plate.

She blinked at him, unsure how to respond. He didn't seem to expect one though as he practically inhaled his food, so she followed suit and started eating even though butterflies had taken up residence in her stomach at his statement.

Vincent was basically implying exactly what she'd hoped for in the deepest part of her heart, but hadn't been willing to admit even to herself. It sounded like he wanted her in Miami. That was good, right? It had to be. Still, it was a huge decision.

"Food not good?" Vincent's soft voice cut through her thoughts and she realized she was just pushing the southwestern style eggs around her plate.

"No, it's great. I'm just thinking." Something she didn't really want to do. Making so many decisions about the future made her head hurt.

"About what?" Now the sensual tone was back and it sent a shiver of awareness curling through her. He'd turned in his chair, swiveling toward her and giving her the full view of that magnificent chest. Sweet Lord, the man was trying to drive her insane.

Food forgotten, she set her fork down and slid off her chair, covering the distance between them in seconds. She could see the faint surprise in his gaze the moment before their lips touched, but it was gone before lust took over.

Grabbing onto his shoulders, she moaned into his mouth as he dragged her between his spread thighs. His hands moved with ridiculous ease as he expertly untied her halter dress and bathing suit top. As both pieces fell down around her body, baring her breasts, he cupped them in a possessive gesture that made her melt.

Arching her back, she pushed into his grip, savoring the feel of his big hands—then a low rumble seemed to almost shake the building. Like a sonic boom or something.

They both pulled back at the same time, but Vincent was tense, his expression hard. "Stay here," he ordered.

Blinking, she frowned as he hurried out of the kitchen toward the hallway. What the hell? She hurriedly started securing her bikini top, then her dress. Moments later he returned carrying a gun. Her eyes widened, not because of the gun—the man was always carrying a weapon—but because she couldn't figure out why he needed one. "What's going on?" she whispered, even though it was just the two of them.

"I don't know, but stay put." His expression was still stony as he hurried to the sliding glass doors. His movements were cautious as he stepped outside, scanning the pool area down below.

When he came back inside, he shut the drapes and started for the hallway. Panic started to hum through her at his tenseness. What the hell was he worried about? Following him, she knew he was aware of her in the hallway because he let out an annoyed growl.

At the front door, he didn't turn around, but muttered a "stay *here*," before he eased the door open. Weapon drawn, he moved outside with a liquid grace, leaving the door only half open.

Quietly, she moved up behind him, but paused when his entire body went rigid and he let out a guttural curse.

A raw, almost burning scent teased her nose. Since she couldn't see anything, she ducked down and peered around his body.

And froze.

In the parking lot below them, dark smoke billowed high into the air above a burning car. *Her car.* Thick orange flames danced along the underbelly and the windows had all been blown out, leaving hideous gaping holes. The stench of burning rubber filled the air, making her feel nauseous. She felt glued to the spot as she stared at the carnage and tried to wrap her mind around what she was seeing.

"My car…"

"Someone blew it up," he said, matter of fact as he propelled her back inside.

For a moment she started to struggle, but he put firm hands on her shoulders and pressed her against the hallway wall. "Jordan, someone blew up your car. I'm not letting you outside. For all we know that was a setup to draw you out. I doubt it, but I'm not taking any chances. We're calling the cops—though I'm sure they've already been alerted—and I'm getting you the hell out of here. And I want to talk to your fucking handler because this kind of attack is personal and it was aimed at you. If there's something they didn't tell you, we're going to find out today." He was practically shaking as he spoke, the anger emanating off him potent and dangerous.

She knew it wasn't aimed at her though. A tremor snaked through her body and she was vaguely aware of the sound of sirens in the distance as she nodded. Had her WITSEC handler kept something from her? Jordan didn't want to believe it. But it was possible that her handler had missed something. Okay, more than possible. Now it seemed almost probable. "I'll get the number."

Terror settled deep inside her at the thought that this was somehow connected to Curtis Woods. There was no doubt the man was dead, but what if the Feds had screwed up and his brother wasn't? Or what if this had nothing to do with her testimony against him at all? Any option was terrifying because she was basically fighting an unknown threat. And she'd unknowingly dragged Vincent into it with her.

Chapter 8

Vincent couldn't remember ever being so angry. Forcing himself to remain calm, he leaned against the doorframe in Jordan's room as she retrieved her cell phone from her nightstand. Her hands shook as she picked it up and that only further enraged him. He hated seeing her scared.

Whoever had destroyed her car was clearly targeting her and he was going to keep her safe, no matter what it took. And make her would-be attacker pay. He was certain that violent fire bomb attack last night was related to her car exploding. There was no way it was a coincidence and even before the police confirmed it, he knew that explosion wasn't an accident. So that left a hell of a lot of questions.

Jordan closed the distance between them and started to hand her cell phone to him, but then snagged it back, her expression pinched. "Her name is Edith Clark, but…I should call her first, explain what's going on."

Nodding tightly, he waited as she scrolled through her numbers then pressed *send* on one of the names. As she held up the phone to her ear he snagged it from her hand, not caring how forceful he was being.

"Vincent," she snapped, but he turned away from her

and strode down the hallway toward the living room as it rang. Stretching his legs released a fraction of his pent up energy, but not much. Beating the shit out of the bomber was the only thing that could do that.

"Hey, Jordan, I was just thinking about you."

"This isn't Jordan. My name's Vincent Hansen and I'm sure you know who I am." As Jordan's handler, this woman would know everything about Jordan's life pre-WITSEC and that definitely included him. Not to mention he was pretty sure someone had helped her out in locating him.

"What's wrong? Why are you calling from Jordan's phone? Where is she?" The woman's soft voice instantly became hard, the change immediate.

"She's right next to me and what's wrong is that someone tried to fire bomb her and me last night and then this morning, her fucking car exploded. Now why don't you tell me what the fuck is going on? Did Curtis Woods have more friends or relatives you idiots forgot to tell her about? This isn't some random act of violence and I want to know every fucking thing about the Woods's case. Now!" He was full on shouting, unable to contain his anger any longer. He knew he should be a hell of a lot more diplomatic instead of pissing this woman off, but he felt like a powder keg. Keeping his cool and staying in control was never a problem—unless Jordan's life was in danger.

"Is Jordan all right?" There was real concern in the woman's voice.

It was the only thing that tempered Vincent's anger. "She's fine, though she's glaring daggers at me right now."

Jordan leaned against the outer kitchen counter, watching him restlessly pace along the tile floor.

"Can you tell me exactly what happened? Are the police involved?"

"We made a report with Detective Leon Hough of the Key West Police Department last night, but then I was operating under the assumption the firebomb was a random act. A driver on a moped threw a Molotov cocktail at us. Her car, however, was just bombed or rigged to explode about five minutes ago. We're holed up in a condo and not leaving until the police have arrived and cleared the area." And he was armed. He already had one weapon tucked into the back of his pants but he'd also retrieved another one and had strapped it to his ankle. "Jordan was under the impression that Curtis Woods and his only living relative were dead. Is that not the case?"

There was a slight pause. "We didn't conduct the investigation of Corey Woods's death. That was done by the Abilene PD and we had no reason to believe their assessment was wrong."

Vincent snorted. "Clearly you guys missed something because someone wants Jordan dead. Two violent attacks in a twenty-four hour period—not a coincidence."

"I'm going to personally check with the Abilene PD and I'm also sending someone to pick Jordan up until we figure this out."

"Over my dead body. She's not going anywhere with you." Unless she agreed, there was no way they could force her into custody either. Vincent kept his gaze on Jordan as he spoke, daring her to defy him. He would kidnap her to keep her safe if he had to. He'd lost her once, he wasn't doing it again.

Jordan swallowed hard and didn't respond. And damn it, he couldn't get a good read on her emotional state. Her hazel eyes were filled with worry and fear, but something else he couldn't define.

"Mr. Hansen—"

"Save it. As soon as we're able, I'm getting her out of

here and we're headed someplace safe. Call her if you need to, but she's not going anywhere with you."

The US Marshal was silent for a long moment. Finally she spoke, her words clipped. "I'd like to speak with Jordan. I need to know she's safe."

Though he didn't want to, he handed the phone to her.

At least her hand wasn't shaking when she took it. Almost resignedly, she put it up to her ear and started talking. Even though she was clearly upset, Jordan stood by what he'd said and told her former handler that she was staying with Vincent.

The knowledge that she wasn't fighting him, that she was willing to stay, soothed something primal inside him. No one would protect her like he could. First, he needed to get her the hell out of here. Then he was calling in for backup.

The second she ended the call, Jordan turned to face him and he could see an argument building inside her before she'd even spoken. "I can't bring any more danger on top of your head, Vincent. I told her no, but Edith is right. Maybe I—"

"Don't finish that sentence," he snarled, covering the short distance between them. He didn't want to hear it. Gripping her slim hips, he tugged her close so that they were toe to toe.

She spread her hands over his chest, the worry in her gaze tearing him apart. "I'd die if anything happened to you because of me." Her words were a bare whisper of agony.

Instantly, the anger that had been building inside of him eased. She was worried about his safety. He couldn't get mad about that. "I know how to protect both of us. I'm taking you someplace safe so we can regroup and come up with a game plan." One that didn't involve hiding or running back to Miami. Not until they figured out who they were up against. "Go pack your bags. Get everything together because we're not coming back here."

"Vincent…" For a long moment it seemed as if she might argue, but she just leaned up on tiptoe and lightly brushed her lips over his. "Thank you," she murmured before hurrying down the hallway.

He started to follow after her when there was a hard knock on the door. Before he'd taken two steps, someone said, "Police, open up."

Vincent had known the cops would be talking to everyone in the building, he just hadn't expected them to reach their condo so soon. After peering through the peephole, some of his tension eased. He opened to door to Detective Hough and a uniformed policeman.

He nodded once. "Detective."

The older man looked past him, down the hallway. "When I got the address of the bombing, I headed over. Recognized it as the complex where Ms. Alvarado was staying."

Vincent glanced down at the parking lot to where firefighters had the blaze almost extinguished and the police had cordoned off the entire area with yellow tape. There were at least a hundred onlookers across the street and people from the condos had stepped out onto their front balconies and were staring at the scene in horror and curiosity. "It's her car that was bombed. We need to talk. Alone." He looked pointedly at the uniformed officer, who frowned in response.

But one look from Detective Hough had the man backing down. Hough nodded and stepped forward. "Let's talk."

"You want some coffee, Detective? It's already made," Vincent said as he shut the door behind him.

"Sounds good. Where's Ms. Alvarado?"

Jordan's head popped out of her room. "I'm in here

packing. Vincent..." She trailed off but there was a question in her eyes.

He nodded, understanding her completely. It had always been like that between them. Sometimes they could communicate without saying a word. Of course now it didn't take a psychic to figure out what she needed. She wanted him to deal with the police. "I've got this covered."

Relief flooded her expression before she disappeared back in the room.

"You guys going somewhere?" the Detective asked casually, though there was nothing casual in his rigid stance.

"As soon as we can pack. Jordan was in WITSEC for seven years." Vincent decided not to play games with the man. Getting right to the point was the smartest thing he could do in this situation and it would likely ensure more cooperation. Hough had been straight with him so far.

The other man's dark eyebrows rose at that and he motioned to the coffee pot as they entered the kitchen. "You mind?"

Vincent shook his head and started gathering the plates. "What's the situation like down there?"

He shrugged. "Ordered chaos. We've got it under control, and the bomb dogs have secured the parking lot and are in the process of doing the same to the perimeter and the building, but the locals are freaking out. The news stations will be descending soon if they're not already here. So, that was Ms. Alvarado's vehicle? You're sure?"

"Yeah, I'm sure. Don't know who did it though." But he planned to find out. Vincent hurriedly gave the detective a rundown of everything he'd learned so far; from Jordan's years in WITSEC, to the names of the man she'd put behind bars and his alleged accomplice brother—who may or may not be dead. Since she'd left the program of her own free will and the man she'd put behind bars was dead, Vincent was almost a hundred percent certain he was legally allowed to divulge this information. Especially since she'd come clean to all her friends about her real identity. Even if he hadn't been allowed to, he would have told him because the detective might be able to help Jordan. That was all that mattered.

When Vincent was done, Hough was silent for a long moment as he digested everything. "You spoke to the Marshals?"

"Yeah. They don't know what they missed, but her handler is scrambling to look into it. I'll give you her information, but we're leaving as soon as we can. I want Jordan away from here."

That information didn't seem to please Hough, but he nodded. "You leaving town?"

"No, I'm taking her to my place. You've got the address in your file. It's more secure and until we get a handle on this situation, I don't want to just blindly run out of town."

"You'll have to make an official statement about her vehicle, but I'll take care of that. I'll also have an officer escort you out of here. Often bombers like to stick around and look at their handy work, so we've got eyes on the area."

Vincent nodded, already knowing that. Bombers, arsonists, and even serial killers loved to see law enforcement scrambling amidst the destruction and chaos they'd caused. They got a thrill from it. It was like sick-fuck 101—they all subscribed to the same messed up handbook. "Fine with me. As soon as she's done, it'll take me a few minutes to get my stuff together."

The detective's radio went off with a request for assistance. After a brief reply, the man set his half empty coffee mug in the sink. "Thanks for the coffee. I'll leave an officer outside. When you're ready let him know and we'll get you guys out of here. Just…whatever you're planning, let us handle it."

Vincent kept his expression purposefully blank. "I'm not planning anything other than keeping Jordan safe. I don't know who did this and I'm not going to take the law into my own hands." Much. He wasn't going to sit idly by and let this threat come to them. Hell no, he had resources and wasn't afraid to use them.

Even though he nodded, Detective Hough still looked skeptical. Once the man was gone, Vincent found Jordan in her bedroom making her bed.

"I'm going to hire someone to come in and clean and do laundry once we're gone because I'm not leaving Barbara's place like this, but I think I've got everything packed up." She nodded to the two red suitcases and matching toiletry case at the foot of the bed.

A ghost of a smile touched his lips. She was worried about cleaning when someone had just decimated her car. "Good. Give me a few minutes and we'll clear out of here."

* * * * *

Stupid fucking blasting caps! Unsure exactly what had gone wrong with the bomb, in the end, it didn't really matter. The fact was, Jordan's car had exploded way too early and without any provocation and that stupid bitch hadn't been in it. In fact, no one had been injured if the layout of the crime scene was any indication.

Cops, firefighters and other men and women in suits who could be with any number of government agencies all milled around the bomb site, but the ambulances hadn't left and no one was being treated. And the medical examiners had already come and gone—without any corpses.

Killing extra civilians would have been somewhat appeasing since Jordan hadn't been injured, but even that hadn't happened. Working without a partner was too hard. Especially when said partner had been the bomb and fire expert. Fire was so beautiful and erotic to watch, but getting it right was just too damn difficult. Maybe it was time to recruit another partner.

It would sure beat working alone.

Blending in with the crowd of tourists and locals across the street was easy enough, but it was never smart to stay for too long. The cops would be watching for anything out of the ordinary and might even take pictures of the onlookers.

And I'm not getting caught by those pigs.

Besides, tracking Jordan with her cloned phone was easy enough, so if she left the condo—and it was likely she and half the residents would be clearing out by the end of the day—she still couldn't hide.

Nope. No matter where Jordan went, tracking her was child's play. Soon enough, she was going to find out what real suffering was. The car bomb might have detonated early, but this wasn't even close to over.

Chapter 9

"Your family owns this?" Jordan asked quietly as the iron gate shut behind the police officer who had driven them to his family's home.

Vincent waved at the guy as he left in his cruiser. "Yeah. It was in my dad's family forever and when he died, he left it to all of us in his will. Me, my sisters and my mom. Probably so no one could ever sell it." Something his dad had likely counted on.

Family had been everything to his father, especially after his wealthy parents basically shunned him for marrying a poor, black Jamaican, second-generation American. His mom had apparently had three strikes against her before she'd ever met her would-be in-laws. His father's parents had ancestors that literally went back to the Mayflower. Elitist fuckers. At least the home they'd given to their son now belonged to those it should.

"This is a seriously nice location and a beautiful home." She sounded awed as she looked around and he loved that she appreciated the area.

The foliage was thick and lush, everything an island home should be. Palm trees, bushes, bright flowers, and two giant Royal Poinciana trees surrounded their home. The whole family had pitched in to renovate the historic Caribbean style cottage. It had real wood plank floors, hand carved wooden beams and custom designed French doors. Even though the house itself was actually small, with two-bedrooms, a kitchen, living room and garage, it was on upper Duval Street. Prime property whether there was a recession or not. Every year he and his sisters grumbled about paying the property taxes, but they'd never give this place up. Not when it was one of their only links to their dad. They rented it for four months in the winter, but the rest of the year they all used it. One or more of them were always here on the weekends or whenever they could squeeze in a getaway.

"Yeah, plus the security is a lot better than that condo. The wall surrounding the place is high enough that no one sane would try to scale it, and the gate has security sensors on it. If anyone tries to come over it or through it, I'll know. We've also got bullet resistant windows, including the skylights." That had been at his insistence and he'd paid for it. The women in his family thought he was paranoid and that was fine by him. All he knew was, they were safe when they were here and that was all that mattered.

"Wow." Fear skittered across Jordan's face as she picked up her toiletries bag from the bricked driveway where he and the cop had deposited everything.

Vincent hefted up his bag, then extended the retractable handle on her biggest piece. "Just leave that one here. I'll come back for it."

Pursing her lips, she just shook her head and grabbed her other bag. "I'm not helpless, Vincent. I can carry my own stuff."

He just grunted. That might be so, but it didn't mean

he didn't want to take care of her. As they neared the front door, he froze. Since he'd walked to Jordan's last night and they'd walked everywhere from that point on, they hadn't needed his vehicle. It was still in the garage, which was shut—but he hadn't left the drapes in the two front windows open.

And they were pulled back. Tense, he abruptly stopped and scanned the perimeter, hating that instant feeling of being exposed to an attack.

"What is it?" Jordan asked, her voice slightly unsteady.

"Maybe nothing." Yeah right. He dropped the bag and wrapped an arm around her, gently pushing her toward the garage. "Hide behind the side of the house," he whispered as he withdrew his SIG in a fluid, practiced movement.

Before she could comply, the front door flew open. On instinct, Vincent raised his gun but immediately lowered his arm as his sister Zoe walked out.

"It's just me," she said lightly. She raised her arms jokingly as she looked back and forth between him and Jordan with clear curiosity.

Vincent sheathed his weapon in the back of his pants. "What are you doing here?"

"Me? What are *you* doing here? I asked mom and she said you were out of town on *business*."

Which is the tiny lie he'd told his mother so he wouldn't have to answer a hundred questions about why he was suddenly dropping everything and coming to Key West. His mom had told him that the place would be free this week so he hadn't bothered asking any of his sisters. He cleared his throat and looked at Jordan once before looking back at Zoe. Yeah, he did not want to have to explain anything right now.

"I've got a work emergency and need the place. I didn't tell mom because I didn't want her to worry.

It's…not safe for you here, Zoe."

Ignoring, the last part, she snorted, her dark eyebrows raising. "Work related? *Really*?"

"Yeah." In the Navy he'd learned that keeping his answers short and sweet couldn't come back to bite him in the ass later. Never give up more intel than you have to. He used that practice with his family. He picked the bags back up, wanting to get Jordan inside as soon as possible. "Come on," he murmured, for her ears only.

Zoe followed as he and Jordan strode past him. Jordan had already been through enough, he didn't want her to have to deal with his family right now too. Zoe was great, but she could get overprotective of him since he was younger.

As he shut the front door behind all of them, he noticed one of Zoe's small pink overnight bags by the coffee table and a small, black toiletry travel case sitting on top of it. Definitely not hers. He frowned. "Who's here with you?" He knew Zoe dated but it didn't mean he had to like it. And he definitely didn't want to think about her having some guy over for a weekend getaway.

Zoe's eyes widened at the question and for a brief moment, what looked like guilt flashed in her gaze. "No one is *here*. And you still haven't answered anything." Swiveling, she looked directly at Jordan who appeared like a deer locked in headlights as his sister zeroed in on her.

She held out a friendly hand. "Since my brother hasn't introduced us yet, I'm Zoe."

Jordan cleared her throat nervously and gave her a tentative smile as she returned the handshake. "My name's Jordan Alvarado."

At that, his sister snapped. He could see it in the tense lines of her body before she let her temper fly free as she turned back on him. "The bitch who broke your heart?"

Vincent inwardly cringed at her words, his own anger

exploding at that word. "Don't ever call her that."

"Why not? She is!"

In that moment he wanted to kick his own ass for ever telling Zoe about Jordan. He'd been shitfaced and feeling sorry for himself one night and had decided to unload everything on her. His sister had been giving him grief about his player lifestyle and he knew she'd been right. So he'd just laid everything out to her. To give her credit she'd never told the rest of the family, but damn her long memory. Vincent turned to Jordan who looked as if she'd been slapped. He hated seeing pain on her face but he could only deal with one problem at a time. "Will you wait in the kitchen? It's through there." He gestured with a hand, trying to curb his impatience with his sister.

Nodding, Jordan hurried out and Vincent had to rein in his anger. He reminded himself that Zoe loved him and if some guy had hurt her, he'd kick their ass. "I don't have time to explain everything to you right now. The only thing I can say is that I'm handling a tricky situation at the moment. I need you to go back to Miami tonight. It's not safe here for you. Please don't tell the family about this either. I can't afford to have mom running down here and getting caught in the line of fire." The drive back would be over three hours and he felt bad about that, but he needed his sister gone.

At those words, it seemed as if most of Zoe's steam dissipated. "There's really a dangerous situation?"

"Yes. And I can't explain it all to you."

"Fine, I literally just got here anyway." She pulled out her phone, sent off a couple texts, then slid it into the back pocket of her shorts. "Seriously, what's going on?" she whispered. "Why do you have her here? I thought she split on you years ago?"

He scrubbed a hand over his face, feeling exhausted. "It's complicated and I can't get into this right now."

"Fair enough, but I've got questions and you're going to answer them when I call." She shot him a warning look he recognized all too well.

"Good, then you can tell me who that travel case belongs to because I know it's not yours."

She just snorted, picked up the two bags and started to head out.

"Wait, where did you park?" There was only room for one vehicle in the garage and his was in it. But if she'd just arrived, she likely wouldn't have seen it yet. And there was no car in the driveway.

"I didn't, I was dropped off because my friend had to pick up…something. And now my friend is picking me up, but I'm *not* leaving town."

"Damn it, Zoe—"

"No, I'm giving you the place and I won't argue with you about how stupid you are to be helping that woman with whatever she's dragged you into, but I'm not messing up my plans."

Vincent wanted to argue with her but knew it would be pointless. She was the most stubborn woman he'd ever met. Besides their mother. "Fine, just…be careful."

At that, she gave him a kiss on the cheek then hurried out. He followed her, watching as she left through the gate and got into an idling black SUV. He memorized the license plate as it drove away because whatever his sister was keeping from him, he was going to find out.

After locking the front door, he found Jordan sitting at the center island. Copper pots and pans hung from the rack and even without the lights on, the room was flooded with natural light from the skylights above them.

He ran a hand over his hair. "I'm sorry about my sister. She didn't mean what she said."

Jordan laughed, the sound strained. "Yeah she did. And it's fine, seriously. I understand why she'd feel that way about me."

No, it wasn't fine, but he wasn't going to get into that now. His sister was gone and he could focus on keeping Jordan safe. "Listen, I've got to make some calls. I'm going to show you to your room. You can get settled in, then we're going to sit down and go over a few things, okay?" He still needed to contact Lizzy and he was asking another friend for backup because right now he wanted Jordan to have as much protection as possible.

She looked as if she wanted to say more, but just nodded, the strain around her eyes and mouth killing him.

As she slid off the chair and started to pick up her bags, he wrapped his arms around her and pulled her close. Though she returned his embrace, sliding her arms around his neck and laying her head on his chest, she was still stiff. As if she was trying to pull back from him. Whether literally or emotionally he wasn't sure. He didn't care. He wouldn't let her pull back from him either way.

Right now wasn't the time to push her though. She was probably trying to come. to terms with being targeted again. She'd lived for seven years in a state of fear, whether muted or not, and had left a safe program because she'd assumed she didn't have any enemies left. Two violent attacks almost back to back, then to get ambushed by his sister, yeah, she would definitely be feeling the strain. He wouldn't add to it.

Kissing the top of her head, he murmured, "Come on, let's get you settled."

* * * * *

Jordan shut the door behind Vincent and pressed her forehead against the door. Having a breakdown right about now seemed like an awesome idea. Unrealistic and totally weak, but still, awesome.

It shouldn't have hurt so much that a relative stranger called her a bitch. She'd been called worse before and by people that had actually held significance in her life. Not some random woman. But...Zoe Hansen wasn't exactly random. She was Vincent's sister, so she mattered.

On a big level. Vincent loved his family more than anyone she knew. Back when they'd been dating he'd tried to protect his sisters even when he'd been living in a different state. It was that protective streak in him.

Jordan wasn't exactly worried she'd come between him and his family because she wasn't sure she would ever be important enough to do that. Things were still new and tentative between them and with all the bullshit going on right now, it hurt more than Jordan could have imagined that his sister basically hated her. Not that she blamed the woman. Well, she could just add that to the big pile of things she didn't want to deal with right now.

Sighing, she sat on the edge of the platform bed and rubbed the back of her neck. A gauzy, almost sheer peach canopy draped above it, a perfect accent to the light pink and orange hibiscus patterned comforter. A richly colored throw and eclectic pillows adorned the bench at the foot of the bed and the rest of the room was similarly bright without being garish. It was like something out of a showroom. Whoever had decorated it had a good eye.

Standing, she started back for the living room. She didn't need to settle in and didn't want to waste time when she could be helping Vincent figure out who was behind her attacks. More than anything, that was eating at her.

Why, when she'd just started to feel normal again, did some psycho have to emerge from out of nowhere? And why, when she was inadvertently putting someone else in danger? Not just anyone, but the man she was pretty sure she was falling in love with again. Or had never truly stopped loving. When she'd left him, it had ripped a piece of her heart out and it had never fully healed.

Now she just felt raw and vulnerable around him. The man wielded so much power over her even if he didn't realize it.

"Enough," she muttered to herself. She could feel sorry for herself later. As she started to open the door her cell phone rang.

Snagging it from the dresser, her heart rate increased when she saw Edith's familiar number. She answered immediately. "Hey."

"Hey, hon. How are ya?" she asked, her voice holding true concern. In her mid-forties, of average height and very slim, the blonde-haired US Marshal looked so unassuming, but Jordan had seen the woman in action before. Before she'd been moved to New Mexico permanently, Edith had stayed with her in a safe house for a month. They'd gone running, worked out together every day and she'd shown Jordan numerous self defense moves. The woman could kick ass when necessary.

"Ah, okay. Stressed out, but okay." Not really, but now wasn't the time to complain. She knew Edith had to be calling for a reason. "What's going on? Have you found out something?" *Please say yes.*

"Yes, I just wish we'd known this a long time ago. Is Mr. Hansen with you?" Now she was all business.

"He's out in the living room."

"Go find him and put me on speaker. I want to tell you both at the same time what our team has discovered."

"Do you know who's after me?" Jordan asked as she hurried down the hallway, barely able to contain the panic humming through her.

"I do and it's un-fucking believable."

Chapter 10

"How did you even get this?" Vincent asked Lizzy quietly, though Jordan was still in the guest bedroom. He stared at the various feeds popping up on his laptop screen. Lizzy had taken over his computer remotely and given him access to video feeds from local CCTVs she'd hacked into in Key West.

The other woman laughed almost wickedly on the phone. "You don't want to know. Neither does Porter. He says it gives him plausible deniability if the cops ever show up at our door." She snorted as if the thought was ridiculous.

Which it probably was. The woman was brilliant and should be working for a government think tank. Of course, they wouldn't pay her as much as Red Stone Security did.

"I owe you so much. I don't even know how to thank you," he said as he started working his own magic. He might not be a skilled hacker like Lizzy, but he was good enough and had fast fingers. In the Navy, before he'd gone through the hell of BUD/s and become a SEAL, he'd been with a small intel unit and had learned his way around computers.

"You don't owe me anything except maybe babysitting duty."

"Deal... How long will I have access to these?" His fingers flew across the keyboard as he punched in commands for the first screen.

"As long as you want. They're not live or directly linked to the sources. I hacked in, downloaded all of them for the past week just in case you wanted to go back a few days in your searches, added them to your computer, then I covered my tracks. There's no trace I was in any of the systems—and most won't have the capabilities to even realize someone was there anyway. We're talking gas stations and single owner businesses. The banks might notice a tiny glitch—"

"Lizzy!" He wasn't trying to be rude, but he knew if he didn't cut her off now she'd never stop. He couldn't concentrate with her talking and he didn't need the details. He knew the basics—she'd hacked into any business that had a wireless—translation, hackable—CCTV monitoring the streets on or around where he and Jordan had been attacked and near the condo where her car had been bombed. Considering how many businesses there were around the vicinity, that was a lot of videos. Of course not every place had live feeds and some recordings recycled every forty-eight hours, deleting the older videos. So he was working with limited angles and feeds but it was a hell of a lot more than the cops could hope to get. They'd need search warrants or permission to see any privately owned businesses' security videos.

Not this way. He and Lizzy were just cutting through all the bureaucratic bullshit as far as he was concerned. And the truth was, the police didn't have the resources to do what was necessary. For the car bombing, they actually might make an exception and hit their investigation hard, but this wasn't like television. Investigations took a lot of time and in some cases, lucky breaks. They couldn't just take video feeds from any business they wanted.

Unlike him.

"Call me if you need anything else. Once you've got what you need, delete all those feeds. I've left our connection open though. Text me when you're done and I'll wipe your computer," Lizzy said.

"You're the best and I definitely owe you babysitting duty. As much as you want."

"I hope she's worth it." There was a slight note of concern in her voice.

"She is." Without a doubt. Jordan was worth risking everything for. "Talk to you later."

Once they disconnected he set his phone on the coffee table and continued scanning a feed from a gas station around the corner from where they'd been firebombed. It was in the direction the moped driver would have gone. Vincent fast forwarded to right after they'd been attacked. Sure enough, a black clad, completely covered individual flew by the first screen a few minutes later.

From there, he cross-referenced the map he had of downtown Key West with the various businesses Lizzy had hijacked videos from. Since he didn't have feeds from every place, there were missing spaces of time, but the moped kept appearing in clip after clip until finally it disappeared into a parking garage of a hotel. Unfortunately he didn't have any access to the garage. Since Detective Hough had already informed him that the license plate number Vincent had given him belonged to a moped reported stolen, he doubted the driver was staying at the hotel. Still, he made a note of it and planned to tell the detective about its location as soon as he was finished. They might get prints off it, though he doubted it. The driver had been wearing gloves and was obviously careful.

Since he had two visuals at different angles from two different video streams across the street, he fast forwarded in the hopes that someone would exit. There were likely other exits and it was a shot in the dark that he might spot the driver leaving, but he had to try.

Scanning through the next hour of footage, only five people left through that entrance. Two sets of couples and a petite blonde wearing a skimpy summer dress. Vincent scrubbed a hand over his face and let out a growl of frustration. Of course it wouldn't be that easy.

As he started to pull up a video from the day of the bombing, Jordan strode into the room carrying her cell phone, her face pale. Immediately, he stood. "What's wrong?"

She shook her head. "I'm not sure yet. Edith is on the phone and wants to talk to both of us." She held it out and the agent's crisp voice came over the line.

"Mr. Hansen, Jordan…" The woman let out a long sigh. "Jordan, I'm not making an excuse for our oversight and I won't get into how the fucking Abilene PD dropped the ball because of typical non-sharing bullshit, but it turns out Curtis and Corey Woods had a half-sister. She wasn't connected to Curtis in any way that we've discovered, but in the course of the investigation into Corey Woods' death, the Abilene PD found out about the existence of a Celia Olson. Now, we have no idea if she was in any way involved with either brother, but she owned a house with Corey ten years ago in a small Texas town. Around that time…there were a string of unsolved fires. A few homeless people died. There might be a connection, but—"

Vincent cleared his throat. "Do you have a picture of her?"

"Yeah, sending it to both your phones now. Like I started to say, she might not be connected to Curtis's crime spree, but I don't like that this is the first we've heard of her."

"What have you been able to find out about her?" Jordan asked, a sharp pop of annoyance clear in her tone.

He didn't blame her for being angry. This is the kind of information she should have had before she chose to leave the WITSEC program. She should have been aware of all potential dangers.

There was a long pause. "We're still gathering data on her, but as of now we haven't been able to locate her. She's officially off the grid."

Vincent didn't like the sound of that at all. Not to mention it was starting to sound like Edith wanted to cover her ass. *Still gathering data.* He called bullshit.

His phone dinged, signaling the message the agent had sent. When Celia Olson's picture appeared on his screen, his heart rate kicked up a notch. He couldn't believe it. He'd seen that face before. Turning the phone to Jordan so she could see, he asked the agent, "Do you have anything we can actually use?"

"We'd like to bring Jordan into our custody until—"

Vincent ended the call.

Jordan's eyes widened as she turned to glare at him. "Vincent, why'd you do that?"

"Your handler doesn't have any more information for you and no one can protect you the way I can, so going into custody is not an option. Besides, Celia Olson is in Key West and I'm going to hunt her down."

Chapter 11

"Hunt her down? Are you out of your mind?" Jordan couldn't stop herself from shouting. "First of all...wait, she's in Key West? You know this for a fact?" If the woman was in the same city that was very, *very* bad. It wasn't a coincidence and unless Jordan had another enemy, then Olson had to be the one behind the attacks.

Vincent nodded, his expression grim as he motioned toward his laptop.

She sat with him on the couch and waited as he typed in some commands. Some kind of video popped up. "What is this?"

He actually looked guilty as he cleared his throat. "It's copies of security videos from local business around town."

"Your hacker friend got these?" Jordan wasn't sure she wanted to know the answer.

He just shrugged and focused back on the computer screen. Moments later, he'd brought up a clip of the same moped driver who had attacked them the other night. "Watch this," he murmured. Different screens popped up, showing various shots of the bike moving across town until it disappeared into a parking garage. His fingers flying, Vincent typed in more commands, then fast forwarded about half an hour into that video according the time stamp. Then he pressed play. "Tell me if you recognize anyone."

A few minutes later a pretty blonde walked out of the garage. Her hair was pulled back into a ponytail and she wore a tight, skimpy dress. She looked left, then right before heading right at a fast pace. Even from a video taken across the street, it was easy to see it was the same woman from the picture Edith had sent them.

"She has to be the person who firebombed us, right?" Jordan wasn't sure why she was asking when it was so obvious.

"And bombed your car." His voice was tense, matching the taut lines of his body.

"So what are we going to do?"

"*We* are not going to do anything," he muttered as he pulled out his cell phone. With those crazy fast fingers, he sent off a couple texts. After he received a few dings in reply, he made a grunt that sounded positive before he sent off another string of texts.

It was hard to tell though because he was shutting her out. She didn't think it was intentional, he was just really focused on his phone. Placing her hand over his, she squeezed. "What are you planning or thinking? Who are you texting?"

He looked up, clear determination in his gaze. "I've got a friend coming in from Miami to watch you. I won't leave you unprotected."

"Watch me for what? You're not leaving by yourself." She would make sure of that.

His jaw clenched and that fierce protectiveness she recognized too well flared in his pale gaze. "My friend is going to watch you and I'm going to work with Lizzy to see about tracking this woman down. Olson might have fallen off the grid but she's staying somewhere and she's not smart enough to stay off security feeds."

"Because most people would never think of that." Jordan certainly wouldn't.

"Exactly. And most people don't have the kinds of friends I do. We're going to find her."

"Why can't you just give all this information to the police?" She didn't want Vincent getting any more involved in this than he already was. She'd already lost years with him, she wasn't losing him again.

"I obtained all of this illegally. Very illegally. And what I'm planning to ask my friend to do again is also illegal. Besides, even if I did go to the police with what we've got, they don't have the resources to dedicate every waking moment to finding this woman. I do."

"Okay, say I'm okay with you locating Celia Olson. When you find her, will you involve the police then?" Even though Jordan knew Vincent would have no problem taking care of the woman any way he deemed fit, Jordan wasn't okay with that. Not because she cared about some monster who'd tried to kill her twice but because she didn't want Vincent to ever be in a position to go to jail. Not because of her. Not ever.

"Maybe." There was a bit of truth in his voice, which somewhat soothed her.

"Who is this friend coming to help you out?" Or watch her, like she needed a babysitter.

He shrugged. "A guy I work with."

"Could you be more vague?"

A slight grin tugged at his lips. "Probably."

He had that wicked smile that drove her crazy. No doubt he knew what he was doing because he wanted to deflect the subject. "You're maddening... How long until your friend gets here?"

"He's coming from Miami so three, three and a half hours. Depending on traffic. And I can think of a lot we can do in that time."

His words took her completely off guard. "You don't need to call Lizzy?"

"I do." His heated gaze narrowed on Jordan's lips.

"Damn it, Vincent. We need to think about this more. You can't just—"

Reaching out, he tugged her so that she was straddling him. Her dress pushed up against her thighs as she slid right over his hard length. The clothes between them might as well have been nonexistent. Lord, he must have gone from zero to ready-to-go in seconds. There was no way they were doing anything until they talked more though. She braced her hands on his shoulders to hold herself away. "If this woman is truly after me, she has to have been following us. Obviously, or she wouldn't have known which car was mine or where I was staying. What if she tracked us to your family's place or—"

"Tracked us," he muttered. The lust that had been simmering in his gaze dimmed as he reached around her and grabbed her phone from the coffee table.

She tried to slide off him but he held her firm, one hand wrapping possessively around her hip, his fingers digging into her.

"I like the feel of you on top of me," he said as he popped open the back of her phone.

With what had happened with his sister earlier and how raw she'd been feeling, that simple statement soothed her in a way she hadn't realized she'd needed. She watched as he first pulled her battery out, then a small black plastic chip that looked similar to her SIM card. But it wasn't the card because that was still in her phone. And that piece was white and pink.

"Son of a bitch." He held it in his palm in between them.

"What is it?" she whispered, though she wasn't sure

why.

"This is a tracker. It's how she followed you. Which means she had to get close enough to you to take your phone and put it inside."

At that realization, Jordan could feel all the blood drain from her face. The woman who'd thrown a firebomb and actually blown up her car had somehow taken her phone off her person. The woman would have been very close to do it. She normally kept her cell in her purse and she almost always had a purse with her.

"Baby, I'm sorry," Vincent murmured before setting the plastic piece down and wrapping his arms around her waist.

She swallowed back the tremor of fear as she returned his embrace, loosely setting her hands on his shoulders. "It's better we know now. Do you know what kind it is? Can she hear us?"

He shook his head and relief punched through her. "No, I've seen this kind before. It emits a signal to whoever is tracking it and uses your phone battery to stay charged. It's mid-grade. Definitely not the cheap stuff, but she could have bought this online or any number of shops. These aren't that common, but finding her through this purchase would be next to impossible."

"So this doesn't help us?" Great. The woman definitely knew where they were and they couldn't use the one piece of evidence they'd found to prove that someone had been following her.

"I didn't say that. I'm definitely going to be able to use this against her." There was a dark edge to his voice.

"How?"

When he just pursed his lips together as if he didn't plan to tell her she pinched his nipple. His eyes widened in surprise as he tried to scramble away from her so she twisted the sensitive skin. "What are you planning?"

"Damn woman, let go." He grabbed her wrist but she

refused to release him.

"Tell me. I can tell you're planning something."

"Fine, fine, I'll tell you." He lightly squeezed her wrist so she released him, but didn't move off him. "I don't remember you being so violent," he muttered as he rubbed a hand against his chest.

"That didn't hurt. Now tell me or I'll squeeze something even more sensitive and you won't like the end result."

"Is it wrong that this violent streak of yours turns me on?" There was an uneven quality to his voice, the question coming out ragged. He rolled his hips once, letting her feel his hard length.

Having him aroused between her legs made her entire body pulse with need, but nothing would dissuade her from getting her answers. "Vincent," she said warningly.

His big hands settled on her hips, his expression frustrated. "I don't have an exact plan, but if this morning is any indication, her violence has escalated which tells me she'll be coming after you again soon."

Instinctively Jordan looked over her shoulder out the big front windows. The drapes were still pulled back. Sitting with him she felt safe, but she knew that was an illusion.

He squeezed her hips so she turned back to face him. "Short of her using an RPG, she's not getting in this house. All the sensor alerts are linked to my phone and the security company so if someone breaches the property, I'll know and so will the police. As long as you're under this roof, you're safe."

"We can't stay here forever." She wouldn't mind staying cooped up under any roof with Vincent, but the reality was that he had a job and a life and they couldn't just wait around and hide because some maniac wanted to pick them off.

"I know. I'm going to take care of your problem. It

might not work, but I'm going to take that tracker to a remote enough place that she might feel comfortable following. Or, I'll drive around Key West with your phone and have Blue following me to—"

"Blue?"

"My friend who's coming to help out."

"His name is Blue?"

"It's his last name…Listen, I don't have all the logistics planned out yet. I'm still thinking, but I will be able to use this tracker to our advantage somehow."

"I'm not letting you go off by yourself." Hell no. He was out of his mind if he thought that. She might not be as skilled as Vincent in a lot of areas, but she wasn't helpless. She could defend herself well enough and she knew how to fire a weapon. Not to mention she'd taken down a serial killer with a Taser and even though it had terrified her, she'd testified against him in court and had given up her life to put the man behind bars.

Vincent watched her carefully, his gaze intense as it swept over her face, narrowing on her lips. When he ran his tongue over his bottom lip in a move no doubt meant to be sensuous, her fingers dug into his shoulders. He hadn't agreed with her yet that he wouldn't be going off alone and she needed to hear the words.

He seemed to have other plans as he slowly leaned forward, his intent clear.

"Not done…talking," she whispered before his lips touched hers.

He pulled her bottom lip in between his teeth, nipping and teasing her in sweet little strokes that had her nipples tightening against the soft fabric of her dress. She'd taken off her bathing suit top earlier and had opted not to wear a bra because the dress had one built in. It would be so easy to reach up and— As if he read her mind, Vincent's hands slid up her hips, waist, and he didn't stop until he'd reached the tie on her halter dress.

With one pull, the tie fell free and the two straps loosened, falling down to reveal her bare breasts. Vincent groaned. "You drive me crazy, woman." He'd barely finished the statement before his head dipped to her chest.

She told herself to stop him, that they still needed to figure things out, but as his tongue swiped over one of her already hard buds, she closed her eyes and let her head fall back. He alternated between breasts, driving her crazy as he teased her nipples. Each flick of his tongue or thumb had the ache between her thighs growing.

But his pressure was light. Too light. He was definitely teasing her and no doubt knew it. While she loved the stimulation, she wanted to see all of him and feel her bare breasts rubbing against his chest. She loved the skin on skin, being as close to him as physically possible.

After so long without him, she couldn't get enough. Grasping at his shirt, she started to tug it off when he pulled back and did it for her. She was mesmerized by the way his muscles flexed and stretched as he lifted it off and tossed it away. Simply watching his fluid movements was a turn on.

Splaying her hands over his chest, she lightly tweaked the nipple she'd pinched moments before, knowing she hadn't actually hurt him. He gave her a mock growl.

"You probably liked it," she murmured before leaning down to drop her own kisses on his chest. She lightly pressed her teeth around his small nipple and he shuddered. She loved it when she made him lose control and while she wasn't even close to that point, she knew they'd get there soon enough.

"I love everything you do, baby." He slid his hands down the exposed part of her back as she continued to tease him with her mouth and tongue. His fingers were warm against her bare skin. As she explored his chest, kissing over the muscular contours and lines, he fisted the bottom of her dress and tugged upward.

Though she hated to stop what she was doing, she leaned back so he could pull her dress completely over her head. He set it on the couch next to them but never took his eyes from her face. Even though he wasn't looking at her body, she experienced a moment of intense vulnerability. There was something in his gaze that made her feel like she was under a microscope.

"What is it?" She attempted to cover her chest with her hands, but he moved quickly, snagging her wrists and holding them at her sides, still never taking his gaze from hers.

He cleared his throat, his pale eyes unreadable. "This thing with us…"

Oh shit. Her heart jumped in her throat and she suddenly didn't want to hear what he had to say. She didn't even want to guess what it was. She didn't think he was going to end what they had going on, but that sentence had a whole lot of different possible endings and most of them weren't good. What if he wanted to tell her that this thing between them would never be like it once had been? Or that it could never be truly serious? Not after the way she'd left him or the way his sister, and probably most of his family, hated her. What if he could never trust her again?

She couldn't bear to hear any of those words. Not while she was naked sitting on top of him. Okay, she couldn't bear to hear the words *ever*. But definitely not right now.

Moving fast, she kissed him hard, plastering her body against him as her lips intertwined with his. Vincent gave it back just as hard, just as hungry, his tongue teasing and stroking in her mouth. When he sat up, sliding to the edge of the couch, she took the opportunity to wrap her legs completely around his waist.

Before she realized what he intended, she found herself flat on her back on the plush rug in front of the couch, him kneeling between her thighs because she wasn't letting go of him. He blindly shoved the coffee table out of the way as her hands greedily roved over his chest. She couldn't get enough of touching him. His muscles flexed beneath her fingertips as she skated her way down to the top of his pants. As she started working the button free, his head dipped to her breast again and this time he wasn't teasing. The pressure was perfect, the growing heat inside her building faster with each swipe of his talented tongue.

Once the button was free, she tugged on his zipper and slid her hand inside his pants. Completely commando. She grinned as she wrapped her hand around his hard length and stroked once with enough pressure that he groaned against her sensitive breast. The action sent a tingle of pleasure shooting to all her nerve endings. With one hand she shoved at his shorts, suddenly desperate to feel all of him on top of her.

Thankfully he helped her, shoving at them until he was completely naked and the only thing between them was her thong, the thin scrap of blue material that might as well not even be there.

Leaning back, he kneeled between her legs, his cock pulsing between his legs as it pointed up beautifully against his ripped abdomen. His pale eyes seemed almost darker as he stared down at her, his eyes devouring every inch of her body. "Jordan…" He trailed off, clearing his throat as if he was nervous.

"Don't say it," she whispered.

His gaze narrowed on hers as he pinned her in place. She couldn't have moved even if she'd wanted to. "I'm not letting you go again. Ever."

All the distress that had been building inside her as she imagined the bomb he would drop was sucked out of her at his words. Her eyes widened as she fought to find a response, to make her throat work.

"I bought you a ring," he rasped out, seemingly oblivious to the struggle going on in her mind.

She pushed up on her elbows as shock slammed into her. "What?"

"Before you disappeared. I had a ring for you. I..." He trailed off, his expression so pained it was like a dagger to her chest, slicing through her.

No, no, no. She did *not* want to hear this. It was so different from what she'd expected him to say, but it was knowledge she didn't need nonetheless. "Don't tell me that," she whispered, stricken. If she'd known that, there was no way she'd have been able to disappear into WITSEC without him.

He started to respond, but she grabbed him by the shoulders and pulled him back down on her. They could talk later. She already felt ripped open and could tell he did too by his admission. They needed to lose themselves in each other because she didn't trust her voice anymore. Leaving him had been hard, that word such a pathetically weak description for the truth of her emotions, but she hadn't had a clue what he intended for their future. Or if they'd even had one. Yes, they'd loved each other but their relationship had been fresh and new and he'd never said a word about her moving to Miami with him.

That had been one factor that had made her decision easier. Now for him to confess that he'd had a ring, she wanted to punch him for telling her. To pretend she'd never heard it. But she couldn't go back in time and un-hear those words.

As his mouth met hers again, she could feel the untamed energy humming through him. Arching her back, she rubbed her breasts against his chest, the friction exactly what she needed but still not enough.

Her inner walls clenched, needing to be filled by him. She was so wet for him she knew it wouldn't take much to climax. So many years of pleasuring herself alone and all Vincent had to do was look at her and she'd combust. But it wasn't just that. His admission had set something free inside her even as it ripped her open. She was so primed for him, so ready.

She wanted him to take her. And she didn't want foreplay. She just wanted him pumping deep inside her.

One of his hands slipped into her hair, cupping the back of her head in a dominating grip, as if he was afraid she'd leave. Hell no. She wasn't leaving or running. Never again.

She slid one hand around his big body, digging her fingers into the hard flesh of his back as he reached between them. She felt the soft snap of her panties break free. The material was so thin it didn't surprise her. What did surprise her was the tremble that rolled through Vincent as he pulled back.

"I can't be gentle now." His voice shook, mirroring the tremble in his hand as he cupped her mound. He slid a finger inside her, his eyes closing as he felt how wet she was. She was so soaked it was almost embarrassing, but she loved that he could feel how much she wanted him.

Rolling her hips against him, she shuddered and clenched around him. "I don't want that."

At her words, his eyes opened and for the first time since she'd walked back into his life she felt as if she was seeing every part of him. She'd hurt him but he still wanted to claim every part of her. He hadn't said those actual words, but she knew what he meant. He wouldn't have told her about the ring otherwise. The fact that he could forgive her and welcome her back into his life after she'd cut him so deep...maybe she didn't deserve him, but she would fight for him.

Suddenly his finger was gone and he was pushing his cock deep inside her. All the air rushed from her lungs as he filled her. Everything else, her worries and fears, disappeared as he started thrusting inside her. She felt completely consumed by him.

Her inner walls tightened around him and she rose up to meet him stroke for stroke. His thick length filled her, making coherent thought damn near impossible. And when his mouth crushed over hers in a frenzy of kisses, she dug her fingers harder into his skin.

Moving her hands down the length of his body, she gripped his ass tight as he pumped into her. With each stroke inside her, his thrusts grew more and more unsteady. She could feel the need for release building inside him because she felt the same thing. Each time he slammed into her he hit that sweet spot, pushing her closer to the edge. Her inner walls grew tighter and tighter, molding around his perfect length.

When he reached between them and tweaked her clit, she lost it, her orgasm flooding through her like a tidal wave. It surged out to all her nerve endings as her back arched and she ripped her mouth from his, letting her head fall back. The ecstasy continued thrumming through her, her climax intensifying instead of ebbing as he continued thrusting.

She knew the moment right before he let go. His entire body tightened, the muscles in his arms and neck pulling taut before finally he buried his face in her neck and groaned against her, as if he couldn't get close enough. It was something he'd always done and something she'd never tire of.

His breath was warm against her skin as he lightly nipped her earlobe, his body shuddering through the last of his release until finally he stilled on top of her. She wasn't sure how long they laid there, but it felt like an eternity. She didn't mind. With her legs and arms wrapped tightly around him, she could have stayed in his warm, protective embrace all day.

Eventually he pulled back a fraction so he could look at her, his blue eyes piercing. "Mine."

A shiver rolled through her at that word. Yeah. She was his. Always had been.

Chapter 12

Vincent tugged his black cargo pants on, then his boots. He didn't care that it was one of the hottest months of the year. He was wearing dark clothes that covered as much of his body as possible because however tonight played out, he had a feeling he'd need to blend into the shadows.

Jordan had been in the shower, but he'd heard the water stop running about ten minutes ago. He'd been busy making phone calls ever since he'd had privacy, but knew that his window of opportunity would be ending soon. Blue had texted him saying he'd be at his place in the next half hour, but Vincent wasn't sure how that was possible unless his friend had broken every traffic law in the book to get to Key West so fast.

But he didn't care about that now. He cared about keeping Jordan safe and bringing Celia Olson out into the open. He wasn't even sure if his plan would work, if he'd even be able to get her to *follow* the tracker once he was in motion, but he had to try. The woman's violent actions spoke volumes so it stood to reason she wanted to come at Jordan again. Vincent was going to make sure he took care of that tonight. Or try his hardest.

In addition to Blue he'd called in other men he trusted from Red Stone to help, and while he hated asking for favors like this, he'd do whatever it took to keep Jordan safe. Now he just had to lay out his plan and hope she was okay with it. Or at least okay enough that she didn't try to pinch his nipple off again.

She still hadn't responded to his admission about buying her a ring and he wasn't sure he wanted her to just yet. Hell, he wasn't even sure why he'd told her at all. He should have waited until after this whole mess was over, but he'd needed her to know how much she'd meant to him. How much she still meant to him. He loved her, plain and simple. Part of him had never stopped. The only time he ever felt completely whole was when he was with her and that hadn't changed. Even when he was angry at her, being with her just felt right. He didn't want anyone else.

His cell buzzed in his pocket, the alert letting him know the privacy gate was opening. What the hell? His sister understood the importance of staying away from here and he knew the rest of his family wouldn't be coming by. He'd already subtly checked in with them and they were all still in Miami. And no one else had the code.

Tense, he withdrew his weapon from the back of his waistband and hurried from the kitchen to the living room. He eased back the thick drapes a fraction to see outside. It was already dark, but he'd turned on the floodlights so that it illuminated the property, including the driveway.

A dark SUV pulled into the driveway and moments later his friend Blue stepped out. Tall and huge, the man had been drafted by an NFL team over a decade ago but then 9/11 had happened and he'd joined the Marines as an officer instead. Apparently everyone who'd known him had been surprised, but after working side by side with him, Vincent wasn't. Even though Blue had been a Marine he'd been attached to Vincent's SEAL team on multiple occasions for vessel boarding search and seizure missions, among other things. He was too big for cave clearing missions, but that was about the only damn thing the man hadn't been able to do. He'd stayed in the Marines long after Vincent had left the Navy and had only recently been hired at Red Stone. While Vincent trusted him more than most men, he wanted to know how the fuck he'd known Vincent's address or how he'd gotten the code for the gate. He hadn't told him either of those yet.

When he heard one of the bedroom doors shut, he let the drape fall back into place as Jordan walked out from the hallway wearing tan shorts and a blue spaghetti strap top that showed off way too much skin. Shoving back his possessive side, he held a finger to his lips and pointed for her to head back to the bedrooms.

For a moment she looked as if she might argue, but then she nodded and did as he said. As she left, he turned off the alarm, switched off the lights in the house then crept to the front door. He kept his weapon loose at his side as he eased open the front door.

Blue was on his phone arguing with someone as he shut the driver's door. When he saw Vincent, he muttered something too low for him to hear and slid his phone in his back pocket. Dressed in similar attire as Vincent, Blue strode toward him, but Vincent shut the front door and stepped outside.

He wasn't letting the other man inside until he had some answers. "How'd you know the code? And how'd you know where this place is?"

Blue scrubbed a hand over his dark hair that he still wore military short. "Zoe gave it to me."

A range of emotions surged through Vincent as he looked at his friend, then the SUV, but he sheathed his weapon. "You're the one who picked her up earlier. You've been in the city since I contacted you." He wasn't asking.

He nodded, his expression wary. "I would have come sooner, but I couldn't."

He tried to rein his temper in. "You and Zoe?" Yeah, he couldn't ask the rest of that question.

"It's not what you think. She's in trouble and needed my help. She refused to ask you. It's why I'm here with her."

"Zoe's in trouble? What's going on?" Shit, and he'd kicked her out of their family home? He'd thought he was keeping her safer being away from him and Jordan. "And why didn't she come to me?"

"Listen, V, I'm not getting in the middle of anything with you and your family. Zoe needed help, and I think she was too embarrassed to ask you. That's all I can tell you. She'll probably rip off my nuts for even doing that much, but I told her I had to come clean. I don't like lying to you."

"She gave you the code?"

Blue nodded.

"Is she safe now?"

His head tilted to the side, his expression incredulous. "Seriously, man? I wouldn't have left her otherwise. Got an old friend staying with her until we sort out…her issues. He's trained."

Vincent wanted to call her, hell, to go see her and demand some answers but now wasn't the time. Maybe he should send Blue back to his sister. He had other friends arriving soon. They could handle this situation.

"I can see what you're about to say and the answer is no. Zoe practically forced me to come here. I…didn't want to leave her but she said if you were actually asking for help it must be important. She had a few other choice words for how dumb you were to be helping some female and after I pointed out the irony of her statement, she punched me in the arm. So here I am and I'm not going anywhere until your woman is safe."

He nodded once, knowing he'd have to wait to talk to his sister later. If Blue said she was safe, he believed him. "Thanks. Come on, Jordan's inside. I want you to meet her and we can go over the plan."

Once inside he turned some of the lights back on and headed for his and Jordan's room. He found her hiding in the closet with one of his weapons. "Everything okay?" she whispered, her grip tight on the pistol.

He nodded and held out a hand for it. She immediately gave it to him and rushed into his arms. He kissed the top of her head. "My friend's here."

At that she tensed and he knew why. Earlier he'd told her he'd be handling everything by himself and leaving her with Blue. "I can't just stay here while you go off in danger. Not when this whole situation is my fault." The guilt threading through her voice slammed through him.

Stepping out into the room, he placed the weapon on one of the dressers and turned her to face him. "None of this is your fault."

Her expression tight, she placed a hand on his chest. "I brought this whole mess into your life, Vincent. And I'm so sorry. For more than just this, for everything. For leaving, for—"

"Enough with the apologies," he growled, putting his hand over hers and squeezing. "None of this is your fault. This woman has clearly been stalking you. Probably because you put her half brother in jail. I don't care what the reason is. I just don't want you blaming yourself and I don't want to hear you say you're sorry again. I *need* to help you, so let me. Please." She belonged to him and he took care of his own.

She nodded slowly, but he could still see the hesitation in her eyes. "Okay, but don't shut me out. I want to help."

He didn't want her anywhere near what he had planned, but he nodded anyway. Though he wouldn't shut her out, he wasn't letting her be physically involved in this in any way. Hell no. "Come on. Let's go over the plan and you can tell me what you think."

* * * * *

Celia Olson watched the steady red blip on her screen. Almost all day the red blip had stayed at one location and it had been too difficult for her to get inside that house or property by herself. The wall had been way too high to climb without anyone seeing her. And right now she had to be invisible. She couldn't afford to make any mistakes, and getting noticed by a random witness was stupid and something she refused to let happen.

It was how her brother Curtis had been caught. Because of a stupid mistake. He thought he could kidnap that clothing store owner with no backup so instead of waiting for her, in his arrogance, he had gone alone. And gotten taken down by a single woman with a Taser. The only smart thing Curtis had done was lie to the Feds and tell them their brother Corey had helped him in kidnapping and torturing all those women. Corey hadn't been involved at all. He'd been terrified of both her and Curtis. Sure he hadn't minded robbing people with her all those years ago, but simple robbery was where he drew the line. When she'd wanted to involve him in other things he'd called her a sick pervert and kicked her out of his life.

She'd planned to kill him then, but he'd known. It was why he'd been in hiding for so long until she'd finally managed to hunt him down and kill him a few months ago. He'd been so wasted that shoving that knife in his gut had been child's play. Leaving him to bleed out behind that bar in Texas had been the perfect way to dispose of him. She thought it was what Curtis had wanted but after she'd murdered Corey, Curtis had killed himself in prison.

Supposedly.

She still didn't believe that. There was no way her brother would have offed himself. It had been virtually impossible to stay in touch with him over the years. Occasionally she sent him letters under the guise of being one of his groupies, but she'd never known for sure if he'd recognized the letters as being from her. Because he'd never responded to any of them.

That had stung but she knew he'd just been looking out for her safety. Otherwise he would have given her up a long time ago. She still didn't like that he'd given the authorities the location of so many of the women they'd murdered but at least he'd kept one to himself.

One unmarked grave she could visit whenever she wanted. Feeling flushed, she squirmed in her seat as she thought about visiting it as soon as she was done with Jordan. If Curtis was here he could have had fun with Jordan before killing the bitch, but Celia just wanted to be done with her.

After the mistake she'd made with the car bomb, she didn't want to bring any heat down on herself. Across from the marina where Jordan had gone, Celia sat in a deserted motel parking lot and decided to suck it up and take care of the woman once and for all.

Then she could leave Key West and pick up where she and Curtis had left off. Not that she'd ever really stopped. She'd still been killing when she hadn't been hunting for Corey, but it wasn't the same without a partner.

Celia had twisted her hair into a tight bun and wore a summer dress. Under it she had on a skintight yoga bodysuit that ended at the top of her thighs. With a weapons belt strapped across her middle, the bodysuit helped keep it secured in place and the dress was loose enough to cover the bulge. She wasn't sure why Jordan had come to a marina, but she was worried the woman might be trying to leave Key West by boat. If that happened she'd lose the ability to track her for a while. She didn't know anything about boats and couldn't hire someone to follow another one. That would just be odd and draw more suspicion to herself.

After grabbing her oversized purse filled with lighter fluid and multiple lighters, she headed across the street. Keeping her stride casual, she was relieved that there were only half a dozen vehicles in the gravelly parking lot of the marina.

As she neared the docks, she slowed but kept her pace relaxed even though she felt anything but. Her heart was racing double time and she had to wipe her palms on her dress once. Partly from excitement but also from nerves. If Jordan was with her lover, then taking them both out would be tricky. Celia would have to shoot the man first. That would be the smartest move. Disable the biggest threat first. At least she had a suppressor to mute the noise of gunfire. But she'd have to be fast and take him down with one shot.

Music played from somewhere to her left and she could see three boats that had interior lights on in the western area of the docks. But according to her laptop, the boat Jordan was on lay docked on the east side, in a secluded section of the marina. Google Earth had given her a decent aerial view of the layout so she knew where she was going.

Heart racing, she surveyed her surroundings as she walked down the last wooden dock. She'd worn dive slippers as part of her backup plan in case things went wrong. They were silent against the wooden planks except for a few creaks every now and then.

Most of the boats along this dock were too small to live in and none of the interior lights were on except for in one. While she didn't know much about boats, she could see the illumination coming through a curtained window of the fairly large vessel. She could also hear faint music and laughter. Male and female.

Maybe Jordan wasn't leaving. Maybe this was some sort of getaway with her lover. She probably thought she was safe. Celia smiled. She'd followed the tracker on her screen instead of actually following Jordan and it had been obvious the driver was trying to make sure they didn't have a tail. After Jordan's car had been blown up she would have been stupid not to be afraid or cautious.

After one more glance around the secluded part of the marina, Celia reached into her purse and pulled out one of the small white tins of lighter fluid. She popped off the red cap then stepped onto the back of the boat. The water around it didn't even make a ripple. Stepping down into the back of the open white deck area, she started spraying the fluid everywhere, but was careful not to spill any on herself. She covered every surface; over the deck, the swivel chairs, the wooden paneling.

The dull chatter still continued inside as she hurried down the side of the boat. Once she was on the front, she pulled out another tin and emptied it over every surface she could manage. The splashes of fluid hitting plastic and wood seemed to be over pronounced in the quiet night where there was barely a breeze skittering over the water, but those inside didn't notice.

Once she was done pouring out the liquid, a sense of elation surged through her, powerful and potent. She never tired of seeing the beauty of flames eating up everything in its path. No two fires were the same yet they were all just as wondrous.

Moving to the back of the boat, she reached inside her purse for her lighter. She was going to be off the boat when it went up in flames, but she wouldn't go too far. In case those inside managed to escape, she'd just shoot them. Not as much fun, but if she had to do it, she would. Then she'd leave exactly the way she'd come. It would take at least a few minutes for anyone else to see the blaze and that would give her enough time to make it to her car. She'd be ditching it and replacing it as soon as possible though.

As her fingers clasped around the cool metal of the lighter, she couldn't fight the smile spreading across her face. She flicked it on. The small orange flame danced before her eyes, beautiful and hypnotic. Hungry. But before she could toss it onto the back deck, a bright spotlight suddenly shone in her face. She lifted a hand, trying to shield her face.

"Hands in the air now! Drop the lighter!" an angry male voice shouted.

"Hands up now!" Another louder voice followed.

Panic slithered down her spine as she tried to look around. The spotlight was making it difficult but she could see the silhouette of multiple men, some on neighboring boats, and they all held guns. She could also hear and feel footsteps pounding down the dock coming toward her.

There was no way they were taking her in alive.

Feigning surrender, she held her hands up as the shouting continued. But she didn't let go of the lighter. As the steps grew closer, she let her body go lax and fell forward toward the opening between the two tied up boats. She tossed the lighter as she fell.

She heard shots and angry shouts right before she hit the surface of the water. The cool wetness was a rush against her senses as she kicked and swam with all her might. She might not be able to get away but she was damn sure going to try.

Too disoriented to tell how many men there had

been, she knew it was enough that her chances of escape were slim. But if she could take down one of them with her, she'd do it.

Chapter 13

From the safety of Blue's SUV, Jordan watched the live video feed one of the Red Stone men had set up across from the decoy boat they were using to trap Celia Olson. Jordan was still uneasy about the whole situation for multiple reasons. Vincent had to be using a lot of resources. Five of his co-workers had flown down on one of Red Stone's private jets to help him out. That couldn't have been cheap.

And it was all just to help her. She hated that she might be affecting his job somehow. This wasn't a small favor. These men were working together to trap a maniac they knew nothing about. She knew all the men were highly trained but still, anything could go wrong. And the woman might not even show up. She shifted in the passenger seat again, hating being so confined. Realistically she knew there was nothing she could do and would only be in the way, but with Vincent putting his life in danger for her, she felt like she should be doing more to help.

"It's going to be fine," Blue murmured without looking at her. Sitting in the driver's seat, he'd been vigilant in scanning the surrounding area of the parking lot they were in.

The lot was next door to the marina, but they were completely blocked from sight by a metal warehouse that housed boats not in use. The rest of the Red Stone men had parked there too, but Blue's SUV was separated from the rest so that if anyone tried to sneak up on them it would be impossible. Not to mention the big man was armed to the teeth. Even the video feed she was watching had some sort of anti-reflective screen on it so that it didn't put off a glow for anyone potentially watching them to see.

"I know." She wasn't sure if that was true, but she was going to be positive. Everything would be fine because it *had* to be. She focused back on the screen. "I see something," she whispered even though it was just the two of them in the vehicle.

"Yeah, they see her too." Blue tapped his earpiece.

"They're sure it's Olson?" The men had mounted four cameras so Jordan was watching four small screens on an already small laptop. It was difficult to tell much about the individual she saw walking down the dock. But her destination seemed clear; the woman was making a direct line for the boat where Vincent had stashed the tracker he'd found in her phone.

Jordan was still kind of awed by the kind of trap they'd set up; complete with audible recordings so it would sound like people were inside the boat. When Vincent had explained everything to her she'd been impressed by how fast the team of men had been able to move.

"Yeah." Blue's one word answer seemed pretty typical of what she'd seen of him so far. He didn't talk if he didn't have to.

That was fine with her. Right now she was tense and on edge, just wanting this whole thing to be over so they could move on with their lives. She was still reeling from Vincent's confession about buying her a ring years ago. Nothing in the world could completely take her mind off that. Not even this situation.

Eyes glued to the screen, she frowned when the woman tentatively stepped onto the boat. She tapped that video feed to maximize it. The other three immediately minimized, giving her a full view of Olson. Her hair was pulled back in a bun and she looked almost casual as she reached into her purse and pulled out... "What is that?" she murmured, unsure what the small box looking thing was. Even with the full screen, the woman's back was to Jordan and she only got a brief flash of whatever it was.

"Lighter fluid." Blue still wasn't looking at her as he scanned the area, but he was clearly getting updates from one of the men.

"They're just going to let her spray it everywhere?" Jordan asked as the woman started splashing it all over the boat. It wasn't as if anyone was actually inside, but still, she hadn't thought they'd let it go this far.

"This is incriminating evidence. They'll stop her before she sets it on fire and if they don't, the evidence will be even stronger. Vincent wants this woman put away for life."

Yeah, so did Jordan. So if for some reason they couldn't tie Olson to the car bombing or anything else, at least they'd get her on this. Trying to fight the building tension inside her, Jordan watched as a bright spotlight illuminated the woman. Even without audio, she knew what was happening when the woman put her hands up in the air.

But when she suddenly dove for the water and the boat went up in flames a second later, Jordan gasped.

"Shit, Vincent's gone in after her," Blue muttered.

A pure burst of panic launched inside her, making it difficult to breathe as her throat tightened. Without thinking, Jordan threw the door open. The laptop slammed to the floorboards as she jumped outside.

"Jordan!" She ignored Blue's warning shout as she started sprinting across the parking lot. Gravel spewed up under her sandals as she ran. She could hear Blue coming up behind her but she didn't care. Olson was in the water and Vincent was in there with her.

For all they knew she was armed. In fact, she almost definitely was. The woman was clearly unhinged and would have come prepared to hurt them in as many ways as possible. Jordan's heart beat out of control as she reached the edge of the warehouse that stood between her and Vincent.

But Blue raced past her and turned, his hands held up, a weapon already in one hand. "Stay behind me. That's an order." The sharp tone made her eyes go wide.

Under normal circumstances someone ordering her around would annoy her, but he was right—and he had a gun. She couldn't go racing into an unknown situation without help. She took a deep, steadying breath that did nothing to calm her heart and nodded. "I will."

He gave her a nod before peering around the corner of the building. "We're clear. Stay close."

She did as he said, staying only a step behind him as they hurried around the building. In less than a minute they'd made it to one of the connecting docks. By now she could see the fire blazing about fifty yards away. Men were shouting and she could see a couple people emerging from their boats.

"Vincent's got her. He's okay." Blue finally stepped to the side and let her walk next to him along the dock.

She couldn't see him. Damn it, she needed to see him. "You're sure? And we're safe? No more threats?"

He nodded. "The threat has been contained—she's in flex-cuffs. You're safe."

That was all she needed to hear. Taking off, she

sprinted down the rest of the dock, her shoes slapping loudly on the planks. As she neared the scene, she saw two Red Stone men trying to contain the blaze with fire extinguishers and a man she guessed to be a resident of the marina joining in. So far it hadn't spread to any other boats. Vincent was nowhere to be seen.

In the distance she heard wailing sirens that almost drowned out the obscenities Celia Olson was screaming.

The woman was face down on the dock with her hands secured behind her back and her feet tied as well. Someone needed to tape her mouth, Jordan thought, as she scanned for Vincent.

Where the hell was he? Despite what Blue had said, a tendril of fear trickled down her spine until she saw Vincent talking to one of the men she'd met earlier. Harrison Caldwell, if Jordan remembered correctly. They were standing off to the side along a small dock that connected two of the bigger ones that held boat slips. Her heart swelled at the sight of him.

Vincent had his shirt and boots off, both laying on the ground in a soggy heap next to him. His muscular arms were crossed over his chest as he nodded at something his friend said. Jordan didn't care who he was talking to. She took off again, running down the dock and he immediately looked up. No wonder, because she was noisy and making a giant spectacle. And she didn't care.

When she was near enough she launched herself at him, not caring that he was soaked or if she looked like a maniac. He let out a soft grunt as she wrapped her legs and arms around him. At the last second she realized he could be injured but as he crushed his mouth over hers in a dominating, hungry kiss she figured he probably wasn't.

Running her hands over his back and shoulders, she told herself that he was okay and unharmed but it didn't stop the tremor that rolled through her.

Vincent pulled back first, his breathing uneven. "It's over."

Even though the screaming woman jarred Jordan's senses, she knew Vincent was right. It was finally over. "I love you, Vincent. I should have told you earlier but I was afraid. I love you so much it scares me. I don't think I ever stopped and…I know you said no more apologies, but—"

He put a gentle finger over her lips, his pale eyes seeming to glow under the moonlight. "Then don't. I love you too. That's all that matters. We can finally move forward with our lives. Together. I wasn't kidding. I'm not letting you go again."

A sudden onslaught of tears burned her eyes. A life with him was all she'd ever wanted but deep down, she'd never thought it would happen. When she'd come to see him, it had been about getting forgiveness and closure. No matter what they faced now, whether from his family or with Celia Olson, she knew they could handle anything thrown at them. Because she was never walking away from him again. "Good because I'm never leaving again."

Chapter 14

One week later

Over her glass of wine, Jordan watched the wives of Vincent's friends talking and laughing across the island in his kitchen. Well, technically it was hers now, too. She'd officially moved in pretty much the moment they'd returned to Miami. He'd simply refused to let her leave. Not like she wanted to anyway. She still had a ton of stuff in storage but she would get to it eventually. That was definitely not one of her most pressing concerns at the moment.

"Can you believe the way Vincent has been acting all evening?" Charlotte asked almost conspiratorially as she glanced over her shoulder through the sliding glass door where all the men were hovering around the grill.

Curious what the other woman meant, Jordan put her glass of wine down. "Like what?"

Charlotte's head snapped in her direction, her dark eyes widening as if she'd forgotten Jordan was there—which she might have. Jordan had been quiet, trying to get to know all the women individually. So far she'd clicked with Belle, but the other woman was now outside with her husband Grant. And since Vincent's mother and sister were also outside, Jordan had been hiding in the kitchen.

Yes, *hiding*. And she wasn't ashamed to admit it. They were intimidating.

The dark-haired beauty cleared her throat and shot Lizzy a 'help me' look before she glanced back at Jordan. "It's just funny to see him so territorial over a woman. He's practically growling at any man who talks to you, even the married ones. He's never even brought a woman around so I hope you don't mind me saying that it's a little entertaining."

Before Jordan could respond, Lizzy continued. "I've gotta say, I *love* seeing him like this. He's so happy."

Jordan's cheeks heated up. She was glad they thought so because she felt the same way. It was almost too surreal to be with Vincent again. "I am too." When her phone buzzed across the island she snatched it up. Normally she would have just left it in their room, but she was waiting on a call. When she saw Edith's phone number on the caller ID she quietly excused herself.

For the most part everyone at the barbeque knew what had happened to her and what had gone down in Key West so she didn't feel rude by dipping out for a few minutes.

Ten minutes later, she collapsed on Vincent's bed and pushed out a sigh of relief as she set the phone down on the comforter. Her hand shook slightly, but from elation not fear. After the Key West police had arrived at the marina last week and arrested Olson, the Feds had swooped in only a few hours later and taken her away.

With Olsen arrested and gone they'd all been free to leave too. Jordan had felt as if a weight had been lifted from her shoulders, but there had still been a dark cloud hanging over her head as she waited to see what would happen with her crazed attacker.

Apparently California and Texas were now fighting over who got to prosecute her, but that wasn't Jordan's problem. Olson had confessed to being the one who helped Curtis Woods—Curtis had lied about his brother's involvement—in his murderous rampage. She'd also confessed to killing Corey. According to Edith, Olson was so proud of every one of her kills. She'd refused legal representation and wanted the world to know how great she was. Edith had also told Jordan that the woman had a pretty terrible upbringing in the foster system. The stuff of nightmares. But Jordan didn't care. She'd ruined so many lives, Olson wouldn't get any pity from her.

Jordan was just glad to have her life back, that justice was being served and a complete psychopath was off the streets. She didn't care where Olson served her time, though if Texas managed to get her, they'd be seeking the death penalty. At least that's what Edith had told her. Olson's fingerprints had been connected to a string of home invasions and murders over a decade ago.

Jordan wanted to tell Vincent everything she'd just learned but decided to wait until this evening. They had a houseful of people barbequing and enjoying themselves right now.

As a thank you to all the men who had helped her and Vincent in Key West they'd decided to throw a party. Of course, she knew Vincent didn't need an excuse to throw one. She loved seeing him so relaxed and having a good time. Now it was time to put on her party face and return.

Hell, she had a lot to celebrate now. As she stood up, someone knocked on the bedroom door. "Come in," she said automatically.

Jordan froze when Vincent's mom walked in. So far Jordan had been able to make polite conversation with the petite woman, but she'd avoided being alone with her or Zoe. Maybe that made her a chicken but she didn't care.

Swallowing hard, she smiled. "I just had to take a call but I'm heading back out there in case you need privacy." Maybe she just wanted to use Vincent's bathroom or something.

Tanice Hansen gave her an assessing stare, her dark eyes unreadable. Vincent was right, his mom was a little scary. She was a beautiful woman, with flawless skin that made her appear decades younger than she had to be. And she was impossible to read. "I like the changes you've made around the place. It actually looks like someone lives here now."

Jordan hadn't been expecting that. Of course, she didn't know what she was expecting from Tanice. "Thank you." So far she'd only made a few small changes, but Vincent had been living like a caveman and she was adding feminine touches. Lord, the man hadn't even had a wine opener. Thankfully he'd told her she could do whatever she wanted.

Tanice stepped farther into the room, looking around, again with that assessing eye. Lord, what was she thinking?

Jordan tried to think of something polite to say but felt like a deer in headlights.

His mother continued though. "When Vincent told me he was moving in with a woman after only a week I was stunned. But then he told me he'd known you back in California. He didn't want to tell me everything, but eventually the whole story came out about why you left him and what happened in Key West. I don't know why that boy thinks he can keep secrets from me," she murmured, almost to herself.

"Oh." She didn't know what else to say. Jordan had broken Vincent's heart seven years ago then put the woman's son in mortal danger a week ago. If she was a mom, she probably wouldn't be a fan of someone like herself.

Taking her completely by surprise, tears spilled down Tanice's face as she stepped closer until they were only inches apart. Jordan wasn't very tall but Tanice was even shorter. "I know we haven't had a chance to talk alone yet, but I just wanted to say thank you."

Jordan blinked, unsure what she meant. And she hated that the other woman was crying. She wanted to reach out and comfort her, but didn't know if she should. "For what?"

"For not taking my son away. He didn't say it, but he would have gone with you seven years ago. And it would have killed all of us." Her voice cracked on the last word and she pulled Jordan into a tight hug.

The strength behind the woman's grip surprised her but she hugged her back, relieved beyond belief by the woman's acceptance of her.

"I know you don't have family, so consider us yours now," she said softly.

Jordan fought her own tears, swiping at the traitorous wetness as it threatened to spill over. Since she didn't trust her voice, she only nodded.

As Tanice started to pull back, Zoe walked in, an almost mirror image of her mother. She saw them hugging and gave Jordan an almost sheepish smile. "I was hoping I'd catch you alone. A simple apology probably isn't enough, but I'm sorry I called you a bitch. Mom told me what you did and—"

"You called her that? With a mouth like that it's no wonder you don't have a husband yet." Tanice shook her head as she stepped back from Jordan, all her focus now solely on her daughter.

Jordan took the free moment to swipe away the rest of her tears.

Zoe rolled her eyes. "Mom! Do we have to do this now? I'm just trying to apologize."

Before Jordan could respond Vincent strode in. For a moment he looked panicked as he looked between all three women.

His mom started steering Zoe out as she said, "We'll leave you two alone but we'll see you outside in a few minutes."

"Did they ambush you?" Vincent asked hesitantly as he shut the door behind them.

Smiling, Jordan shook her head. "No, I think your mom likes me."

At that, he grinned and closed the distance between them. "Yeah, she might have mentioned something about hurting me if I ever hurt you. For what it's worth, I don't care what my family or anyone thinks of you. I love you, Jordan."

Those words meant more than he could know. She'd been without family for so long and while she didn't need a huge one, she did need him. "I don't think I'll ever get tired of hearing that." She wrapped her hands around the back of his neck, ready to pull him down for a kiss when he dropped to one knee. "What are you doing?" she whispered, her voice ragged as he pulled a small blue box from his pocket.

For a moment she could see the nervousness in his gaze as he popped it open. Her mouth fell open as she stared at the solitaire diamond. She didn't know much about diamonds but it was big and sparkly and there was no mistaking what this was.

"Marry me." His voice was just as ragged as hers had been.

With tears streaming down her face she fell to her knees in front of him and wrapped her arms around his neck in a tight grip. "Yes."

She only let him pull back so he could slip the ring

onto her left hand ring finger. Staring at it, a burst of elation took flight inside her, wonderful and still surreal. She knew it would take a while to get used to not feeling like she had to constantly look over her shoulder. And more importantly, she wanted to embrace just being happy and stop feeling like this new life was going to be ripped away from her at any moment. "It's beautiful," she whispered.

"You're beautiful and now everyone knows you're mine." His voice had taken on that possessive quality that made her insides melt and she knew that if they didn't have a houseful of guests, she'd be flat on her back in the next few seconds. But she kind of liked the anticipation. After so many years without him, she could wait another couple hours.

The End

Dear Readers,

Thank you for reading Protecting His Witness, the seventh story in my Red Stone Security series. After Fatal Deception (book 3), I thought I was ready to write Vincent's story, but he just kept putting me off. I've never had so much trouble with a character. Finally I realized I had to step back and let things develop organically. I knew if I pushed, it wouldn't be the right story. I'm so glad I listened to my instinct and waited because I believe Vincent and Jordan got the perfect HEA that they deserve. I really hope you all enjoyed their story as much as I enjoyed writing it!

For those who have read this series from the beginning, thank you so much for loving this world as much as I do. One of the most frequent questions readers ask me is if I plan to continue this series and the answer is yes! For those who have just discovered my Red Stone Security world, I've included sneak peeks from the first two books so I hope you enjoy them!

Happy reading,

Katie

No One to Trust
Red Stone Security Series

Secrets are what keep a family strong. United. Elizabeth Martinez could still hear her father's words echoing in the recesses of her memories. Over a decade had passed and not a day went by that she didn't wish she could rewrite history. Some secrets had a way of eating a person alive. From the inside out, one giant bite at a time. Gnawing until she couldn't stand it. If her father hadn't forced them all to keep the family's dirty little secret, maybe she'd be at home enjoying a nice glass of wine and a bubble bath. She wouldn't be picking up her brother from a drug dealer's house on a chilly Tuesday evening.

Lizzy put her BMW into park and slid from the vehicle. This particular mansion in Keystone Island was the last place in the world she wanted to be. Unfortunately her brother had called begging for help. Again.

Everyone else in the family had turned their back on Benny but she simply couldn't say no when he needed her. Not when he'd always been there for her.

While she wasn't sure what Benny was doing at the

recently deceased Alberto Salas's home, she knew it couldn't be good. Salas had been infamous for running drugs up and down the entire East Coast. She'd heard his son, Orlando, had taken over his operation. She'd briefly interacted with Orlando at a few charity functions around Miami and he'd always been perfectly polite, but the man gave her the creeps. There were some things an Armani suit simply couldn't hide.

Self-consciously, Lizzy tugged at her dress as if she could somehow make it grow a couple inches longer. The bright turquoise halter-style dress and black cardigan sweater she wore were completely respectable, but as she walked down the stone driveway toward the front door, she could feel several sets of eyes on her. Considering Orlando Salas was rumored to be in the same business his father had been, she guessed that even though she couldn't see them, he had plenty of scary looking security guys milling around. They were nothing more than thugs in suits and ties. She worked for one of the best security firms in the nation and the guys she worked with—they sure weren't thugs. No, they were highly trained, mostly ex-military, and didn't deal with scum like Salas. They protected uber wealthy clients and government dignitaries and everyone they worked for got a detailed military level background check— courtesy of her computer skills—and if it appeared they were into anything like drugs, Red Stone Security didn't take them on. With how much money their company made, they could afford to be picky.

Before she could knock on the bright red door, it swung open and a man carrying an assault rifle looked her up and down.

A cold chill slithered through her, mainly because of the look on his face, rather than the gun. She'd known the guards here would be armed, but *yuck*, this guy made her feel like she was naked. Clutching her purse tighter against her side—as if that could somehow save her— she started to tell him why she was there, but he beat her to it.

With a lecherous grin on his face, he stepped back and allowed her to enter. "Your brother's out back." He pointed down the tile hallway. "Just follow until you reach the French doors."

Fighting back the growing panic humming through her, she nodded and did just as he said. Yeah, maybe she should have called her boss and told him what she was doing but she didn't want to drag anyone she knew into Benny's problems. Then everyone would know how messed up her family really was. It was too embarrassing. She'd take care of it just like she always had. *Chin up*, she ordered herself.

As she neared the doors she could see her brother stretched out on an Adirondack chair. She yanked the door open and hurried to his still form. "Benny!"

When he didn't stir, an icy fist clasped around her heart. He looked like a corpse. His normally bronze face was a grayish color. She touched his wrist and a sharp burst of relief popped inside her. At least his pulse was strong. But his face…tears blurred her vision for a moment. A garish purple bruise covered his left cheek and one of his eyes was swollen almost all the way shut. A light trail of blood had trickled from his nostril and dried on his upper lip. Had they broke his nose? Her throat tightened with raw grief. He'd sounded bad on the phone but she hadn't expected *this*. She wanted to touch him, comfort him somehow, but was afraid she'd only hurt him more.

Her hand hovered over his pale face for a moment before she settled on brushing a lock of his dark hair away from his forehead. "What have you gotten yourself into," she whispered.

"He's going to be out for a little while." She swiveled

around at a familiar male voice and let her hand drop.

Monster. The word echoed inside her but she bit it back. "Mr. Salas." She tried to keep the disdain out of her voice as she faced the man who'd likely beaten her brother. Or at least watched while one of his men had. Somehow she managed to blink back the tears threatening to spill over.

"Please call me Orlando. You're a very good sister to pick your brother up so quickly." Standing about ten feet away from her, he leaned against the mini-bar with a glass tumbler in hand.

She narrowed her gaze. Anger battled with the fear blossoming inside her but she was still level-headed enough not to cower in front of him. A man like this probably craved the fear of others. "Did you do this to him?"

His shoulders lifted in a slight shrug. "Not personally. Benito owes me quite a bit of money and I intend to collect."

"How much?"

"A hundred thousand."

Lizzy swallowed but tried to school her shock. Benny had had problems with drugs in the past but he'd been clean for a while. Unfortunately, he'd found a new drug of choice. Gambling. If she had to guess, he owed Orlando the money because of bad bets. Or maybe he was back into drugs. She just didn't know. And she hated what her brother did to himself. He had such a good heart but he couldn't seem to keep it together.

Her parents had the money. *She* definitely didn't. And it was unlikely her parents would fork over that kind of cash for the black sheep of the family. Unless she could convince them it was for her. Despite the terror splintering through her, she stood her ground. "So you tried to *beat* the money out of him?"

His dark gaze seemed to penetrate right through to

her innermost thoughts. "He's lucky he's not dead. Out of respect for your family, I'm giving him one week to pay me back."

"And if he doesn't?" She hated that the question came out shaky, but she couldn't help it. She was scared, even if she tried to hide it.

"I sincerely hope he has a life insurance policy." He placed his glass on the bar and covered the short distance between them in seconds. Before she could react, he'd pressed her against one of the columns lining the outer edges of the lanai. His breath was hot on her cheek and his expensive cologne nearly smothered her as fear clawed at her insides. "I might be willing to bargain, however, Ms. Martinez. You are a beautiful woman. Six months as mine, and I'll let your brother off." His hips jerked forward and she pushed back the bile in her throat when she felt his erection against her hip.

Instinct overtook her fear as she shoved at his chest. "You're disgusting."

He was immovable. Grabbing her wrist, he pinned it above her head. When she swung out at him with her other hand, he snapped it up with the same precision. She tried to tug against him, but the man's grip was like an iron shackle. Cold sweat blossomed across her forehead and spread the length of her body. She hadn't told anyone where she was going, and Orlando Salas was total scum. If he raped her, he wouldn't let her live to tell anyone. No, he'd likely dump her in the ocean. She racked her brain, trying to think of a way out of her situation when a loud shout and glass breaking inside caused him to let her go. But not before he backhanded her across the face and growled, "Stay here."

The abrupt action surprised her more than it hurt. A dull throb spread across her cheek, but it was nothing compared to what would happen to her if she didn't get out of there. As he started to reach for a gun tucked in the back of his pants, the double doors flew open and the last person she expected to see stormed through, with a SIG in hand.

And it was pointed directly at Orlando.

"Are you okay, Elizabeth?" Porter Caldwell, her unlikely savior, asked in his typical clipped tone.

"I'm fine." At the moment, all that mattered was getting out of there alive. She wasn't exactly sure what Porter was doing there or even how he'd gotten past Orlando's guards. She wasn't going to balk at a chance to escape, even if her rescuer was her sort-of-ex/almost-lover. Even though they'd dated for a month and gotten pretty physical, they'd never actually had sex so she didn't think that qualified him as an old lover.

"Do you know who I am?" Orlando spat, but Lizzy noticed he didn't continue reaching for his gun. He wasn't that stupid.

Porter's pale blue gaze narrowed with deadly precision. "More importantly, do you know who *I* am?" Without waiting for a response, he strode toward Orlando and slammed the gun across his head with a vicious blow.

With a short-lived cry of surprise, Orlando crumpled onto the mosaic tile. Lizzy had expected more of a response from the man but maybe without his security to back him up he wasn't so tough after all.

Porter grabbed Lizzy's wrist and started tugging her toward the open doors. "We have maybe sixty seconds to get out of here before the rest of his guards realize what's going on. I don't know what the hell you're doing here, but—"

She yanked hard against his grasp. "My brother!"

He paused to stare at her, his gaze unreadable. "What?"

She nodded at Benny. "We need to get him out of here too."

His head cocked slightly to the side as if seeing the crumpled heap that was her brother for the first time. Mr. Tall, dark and annoyed muttered something under his breath before tucking his gun away. Then he lifted her brother onto his shoulder as if he weighed nothing. Benny was almost six feet tall but Porter was taller and much broader. And all muscle. "Follow me," he grunted.

Clutching her purse to her side, she hurried after Porter. "What are you doing here?" she whispered.

"Saving your pretty little butt. Ask your questions later. We need to get the hell out of here."

Danger Next Door
Red Stone Security Series

Grant opened his eyes at the sound of his cell phone buzzing across the nightstand. The insistent hum was going to drive him insane. Grabbing it, he looked at the caller ID then shoved the phone under his pillow.

It was Porter. Again.

He loved his oldest brother—okay, his whole family, but he wished they'd leave him the hell alone. If he decided to take the job at Red Stone Security and work with both his brothers and father he'd do it when he was damn well good and ready.

And not a minute sooner.

He rolled onto his side, ignoring the stiffness in his shoulders. Right now he was just trying to keep it together. After leaving the Miami Police Department he felt lost for the first time in his life. Not something he was used to. Right out of high school he'd joined the Marines just like his big brother had done. Four years later after an honorable discharge he'd joined the Miami PD. His first two years as a rookie he'd gone to night school while working as a patrolman. When he'd made SWAT he'd spent the next two years finishing up with his Bachelor's degree in Criminal Justice. And for the last two he'd been working as a detective and he loved it.

Well, *had* loved it.

Now he was on temporary disability and trying to figure out what he was doing with his life. Half a year ago things had been so clear. He'd had his entire life mapped out. Now, not so much.

Forcing himself to get out of bed and to stop the fucking pity party he was about to have, he took a quick shower and didn't bother looking in the mirror before or after. Seeing his scars only reminded him of what a deformed monster he was. No thanks. He thought about it enough and didn't need the visual aids.

Making his way to the kitchen he avoided glancing at picture frames dotting his hallway walls or anywhere else. They were all filled with pictures of his happy smiling family. His brother Porter and fiancé Lizzy. Or his brother Harrison and gorgeous wife Mara. Or his brothers, father and Grant, *before* the accident.

When he'd been a normal guy. Not Hollywood handsome, but good looking enough to get laid on a regular basis. Now...fuck, he hated the bitterness welling up inside him.

He was alive and had a great family. He'd get over it. Just not today. As he started making a pot of coffee he glanced out his kitchen window and into his neighbor's window and froze.

He had the perfect view of his new neighbor. She was beautiful. Scratch that. The word didn't even come close to describing her. There'd been moving guys in and out of the two-story house all day yesterday but he'd had no clue who was actually moving in. Holy shit, if *that* was her he'd probably scare the hell out of her the first time she saw him. Gorgeous women like her did not associate with someone like him. It would only make her self-conscious or worse—pity him.

But she wasn't even aware of his presence so he could drink in his fill right now. Even if he did feel a little like a peeping Tom.

She didn't seem very tall, though it was hard to measure. Her dark wavy hair cascaded down over her shoulders, reaching just below her breasts. Very full breasts. Definitely enough to fill his palms. And the tight tank top she was wearing left very little to the imagination. It was obvious she'd just woken up as she rubbed a hand over her face and reached for the coffee pot.

Look away, he ordered himself.

But he was rooted to the spot. There was a lot of natural light shining into her kitchen from the windows at the back of her house. He couldn't see the other windows from his angle, but he'd been inside the house before his former elderly neighbors moved out, and it was bathing her like she was some sort of goddess.

Yawning, she stretched her arms over her head and showed off a nice expanse of toned, tanned belly and— yep, he was walking away now.

Before he really did turn into some sort of pervert. Time to work out and do his leg exercises and *not* think about the beauty next door. He'd never walk completely normally again but damned if he wouldn't get close. After completely blowing his knee out when he'd tackled that kid, he'd since had two surgeries. Now there was nothing more doctors could do. He had pins in his knee and he just had to work on getting used to using all his muscles again. Spending time gawking at his neighbor wasn't going to do him any good.

A couple hours later he'd worked out his upper body and had spent some serious time on the treadmill. Sure he wasn't jogging, but he wasn't slowly walking anymore either. Knowing when he'd pushed himself to the limit he changed into his bathing suit and found relief as he descended the steps to his swimming pool.

Immediately the pressure on his leg eased, giving him that weightless relief. Floating on his back, he savored the way his muscles pulled and stretched as he slowly did the backstroke. It wasn't quite noon yet, but the sun was high and bright in a cloudless sky. Since it was April there was a cool breeze but spring in Florida was more like early summer than anything. As he glided through the water he paused at the sound of shouting.

Lifting his head out of the pool, his feet touched the cement in the shallow end. A raised male voice came from the direction of next door. Then the sound of a distressed female voice—with a healthy dose of panic.

Hell no.

Not caring enough to stop and cover up he got out of the water. The voices grew even louder. Cursing his limp, he yanked open the door to his privacy fence, then tried his neighbor's. It easily swung open.

For a moment Grant saw red at the scene in front of him. A tall, lean dark-haired man with an olive complexion had his hands wrapped around the upper arms of the woman he'd seen this morning through the window. The woman was struggling against him, her hand on the middle of the man's chest. The bastard only tightened his grip.

"What the fuck are you doing?" Grant boomed, his voice just a notch short of shouting.

The two people froze. When the man looked over his shoulder at Grant his hands immediately dropped, though his expression was hostile. "Who are you?"

"I live next door," he said, lowering his voice this time. "And you didn't answer me."

Relief flicked in the woman's green eyes as she took a not-so-subtle step back from the man, rubbing her upper arms where the imprint of the man's fingers stood out on her smooth skin.

"This is a private matter," the man said, his dark eyes flashing with annoyance.

Grant ignored him as he focused on the clearly frightened gorgeous woman. "Is this man your boyfriend or family member?" Not that Grant really cared because this asshole was leaving no matter what. He just wanted to know what type of situation he was dealing with.

The woman snorted, taking him by surprise. "No. And he was just leaving."

The man swiveled back to her and took a step forward. "Damn it—"

Grant had moved across the few yards before he'd realized it. The man was about an inch taller than him, putting him at six foot three. But he was lean and a little lanky and even with Grant's bad leg he had no doubt he could flatten him. Hand to hand combat was his specialty and something told him that a guy who didn't have a problem roughing up a woman would be a complete pussy up against a man.

Something about Grant's expression must have conveyed he was ready to take him down because the guy lifted his hands and took a small step back, nearly tripping over his feet. "This was just a misunderstanding."

"The lady told you to leave." There was an edge to Grant's voice.

The man shot an angry look at the woman but hurried toward the gate. Once he reached it he said, "This isn't over," as he practically sprinted away.

Staying where he was, Grant ran his gaze over the woman. He tried to keep it clinical, but it was difficult. Petite but curvy, the brunette had her arms wrapped tightly around herself. Now that he was seeing her up close he realized she likely had Mediterranean heritage. Her skin was a smooth, olive complexion similar to the man who'd just left. But her face was incredibly pale, almost ashen.

Not wanting to scare her, he stayed immobile even though something deep inside him told him to gather her in his arms and comfort her. Yeah, he was sure that would go over real well.

Clearing his throat, he said, "I'm Grant Caldwell. I live next door. Are you okay?"

She opened her mouth, those full lips parting— making him think thoughts he had no business thinking—but just as quickly she shut it as she shook her head. That's when he realized her entire body was shaking.

ACKNOWLEDGMENTS

I owe a big thank you to Kari Walker, Carolyn Crane and Joan Turner for their help with this story! And of course, thank you to my readers! Because of you, the Red Stone Security series is still going strong. You all are wonderful and I hope you enjoy this newest installment! As always, thank you to God for being there through the good and the tough times.

Complete Booklist

Red Stone Security Series (romantic suspense)
No One to Trust
Danger Next Door
Fatal Deception
Miami, Mistletoe and Murder
His to Protect
Breaking Her Rules
Protecting His Witness

The Serafina: Sin City Series
First Surrender

Individual Romantic Suspense Titles
Running From the Past
Everything to Lose
Dangerous Deception
Dangerous Secrets
Killer Secrets
Deadly Obsession
Danger in Paradise
His Secret Past

Deadly Ops Series
Targeted
Bound to Danger (late 2014)

Individual Paranormal Romance Titles
Destined Mate
Protector's Mate
A Jaguar's Kiss
Tempting the Jaguar

Enemy Mine
Heart of the Jaguar

Moon Shifter Series (paranormal romance)
Alpha Instinct
Lover's Instinct (novella)
Primal Possession
Mating Instinct
His Chosen Wolf (novella)
Avenger's Heat

About the Author

New York Times and *USA Today* bestselling author Katie Reus fell in love with romance at a young age thanks to books she pilfered from her mom's stash. Years later she loves reading romance almost as much as she loves writing it. However, she didn't always know she wanted to be a writer. After changing majors many times, she finally graduated with a degree in psychology. Not long after that she discovered a new love. Writing. She now spends her days writing dark paranormal romance and sexy romantic suspense. For more information on Katie please visit her website at www.katiereus.com or her facebook page at www.facebook.com/katiereusauthor.

5320145R00092

Printed in Great Britain
by Amazon.co.uk, Ltd.,
Marston Gate.